DEDICATION:

To Nancy, Dylan and Casey.

To Shawn, Gabriel, Gwendolyn and Cooper.

And to the American Dream.

PETER KELLOGG (book and lyrics) has two Tony noms for a musical of *Anna Karenina* (composer Dan Levine), which has toured 3 times in Japan and was broadcast on Japanese Public TV. With David Friedman, he created *Nicolatte and Aucassin,* based on the French romance, and produced at Westport Playhouse, The Prince and Village Theatre; *Stunt Girl,* based on the life of Nellie Bly, which premiered at Village; and *Desperate Measures*, a 6-person western based on *Measure for Measure* which opened at The York Theatre and won Drama Desks for Best Music and Lyrics and the Outer Critics Circle Award for Best Musical.

DAVID FRIEDMAN (music) Theatre: *Chasing Nicolette, Stunt Girl, Desperate Measure*s, *Scandalous, King Island Christmas* (over 40 productions worldwide), *Listen to My Heart* Revue. Songs: *We Can Be Kind, Help is on the Way, We Live on Borrowed Time, Rich, Famous & Powerful* and hundreds more. Film: Conductor/Vocal Arranger *Beauty & The Beast, Aladdin, Pocahontas, Hunchback*. Composer: *Trick, Lizzie McGuire* (double platinum), Disney's *Bambi* sequel. Record producer: Nancy LaMott (CD's & DVD's currently available). Songwriter: Diana Ross (quadruple platinum), Barry Manilow, Laura Branigan, Alison Krauss, many others. Songbook, CD's, info available at MIDDER.com.

MICHAEL X. MARTIN (illustrations) has appeared in the Broadway shows *The Bridges of Madison County, The Front Page, It Shoulda Been You, Curtains, 9 to 5, Bright Star, Nice Work if You Can Get It, Catch Me if You Can, My Fair Lady, All Shook Up, 1776, Kiss Me Kate, Ragtime, Les Miserables, Man of La Mancha, Oklahoma!* And *King David*. He has also been in a dozen Off-Broadway shows, over one hundred regional productions, concerts at Royal Albert Hall, the Manaus Opera House, and Carnegie Hall. Recent TV credits include *The Marvelous Mrs. Maisel, Madame Secretary, Boardwalk Empire,* and the *Law and Order* hat trick. When asked nicely, he draws cartoons.

He's kept his mouth shut long enough.

MONEY TALKS

*A musical that chronicles
the adventures, wisdom and harangues
of a hundred dollar bill*

Book & lyrics
Peter Kellogg

Music
David Friedman

Illustrations
Michael X. Martin

SONGS:

1. I'm money - Franklin, Washington, Hamilton, Lincoln
2. I love you because you're you - Jenny
3. Texas Hold 'em - Floyd
4. Dumb blonde - Brooke & 3 men
5. I'm chasing a dream - Jorge, Juanita, Franklin
6. How did I fall so high? - Juanita
7. Come to Luigi's - Luigi
8. The world runs on money - Franklin and ensemble
9. The Barber of Queens - Francois
10. Give, give, give to the lord - Preacher and ensemble
11. Does anyone hear me now? - Franklin
12. My golden parachute - CEO
13. Overnight - Tom and wife
14. Finale - Franklin, Washington, Lincoln, Hamilton

Cast of four: 3 men and 1 woman.
One man plays Ben Franklin,
the other 3 play everyone else.
Time: recent past
One act: 95 minutes long

WOMAN plays: Alexander Hamilton, Jenny, Brooke Fairbanks, Juanita, Hooker, Lobbyist, Female Lawyer, Arietta Hardcheck, New Hundred, Miss Pennyworth, Sterling Granderson.

MAN 1 plays: Lincoln, Tom Granderson, Ernie LaCoste, Jorge, Thief, Luigi, Congressman Cheezly, Barber, Evan Pryce, Louella Wadsworthy, Teller

MAN 2 plays: Washington, Announcer in Club, Floyd Buckwaller, Jake, Officer Gaines, Congressman's wife, Jeff Pryce, Reverend Wadsworthy, Mr. Swagmore, Moving Man.

       *   *   *

Money Talks was originally produced at The Davenport Theatre in New York City with the following cast:

Ben Franklin .... Ralph Byers
Woman .... Sandra DeNise
Man 1 .... Brennan Caldwell
Man 2 .... George Merrick

It was directed by Michael Chase Gosselin

*"Finding myself to exist in the world,
I believe I shall, in some shape or other,
always exist."*

- Ben Franklin

(Lights up on 4 people in silhouette. Ben Franklin comes to life, steps forward)

BEN:
ONCE I WAS A MAN,
WITH DREAMS AND IDEALS.
MY VIEWS WERE IN DEMAND.
WHEN I SPOKE, PEOPLE LISTENED.
I CARED ABOUT THIS LAND.

(Lincoln (Man #1), Washington (Man #2) and Hamilton (woman) come to life behind him)

ABE:
I WAS FREEDOM'S FRIEND,
ALEX:
DEMOCRACY'S DEFENDER.
GEORGE:
AND HOW DO THEY REPAY ME?
ALL 4:
THEY'VE CHOSEN TO PORTRAY ME
GEORGE:
AS DIRTY,
ALEX:
FILTHY,
ABE:
VULGAR
(They hold up large bills with their faces in center)
ALL 4:
LEGAL TENDER.

I'M MONEY, THE ALMIGHTY DOLLAR.
PEOPLE ROUND THE WORLD ADORE ME.
THEY LIE, CHEAT, KIDNAP, STEAL AND KILL
AND RUN FOR OFFICE FOR ME.

I'M MONEY, MOTHER OF INVENTION,
THERE'S NO ONE WHO DOESN'T WANT ME.
PEOPLE WITHOUT ME STRUGGLE TO LIVE
WHILE THOSE WHO HAVE ME FLAUNT ME.

GEORGE:
EVERYBODY LOVES ME.
BEN:
YES, GEORGE, THAT'S TRUE.
BUT THEY LOVE ME A HUNDRED TIMES
AS MUCH AS YOU.
ALEX:
ALEXANDER HAMILTON WAS KILLED
BY AARON BURR,
BUT NOW I'M ON THE TEN,
WHICH MAKES ME FAMOUSER.
ABE:
I'M A TUNNEL, I'M A CENTER,
I'M INSURANCE, I'M A CAR.
BUT MY PHOTO ON THE FIVE
IS WHERE I'M FAMOUSER BY FAR.

ALL:
I'M MONEY. POWER TO THE PEOPLE.
BAIT FOR EVERY PIGEON.
MEN MAY CLAIM THEY WORSHIP GOD,
BUT I'M THEIR TRUE RELIGION.

I'M ON THE MONEY.
I'M ON THE MONEY.
I'M ON THE MONEY.
I'M ON THE MONEY.

ONCE I WAS A MAN
WITH DREAMS AND IDEALS.

SCENE 1: A Strip Club

(George, Abe and Alex exit. Ben Franklin, as the man on the hundred, is in all the other scenes. He addresses the audience. No one on stage can hear him, just us.)

FRANKLIN: "We hold these truths to be self-evident, that all men are created equal, that they are endowed by their Creator with certain unalienable Rights, that among these are Life, Liberty and the pursuit of Happiness." It seemed like such a good idea at the time.

(Lights up on strip club. We see a very drunk stockbroker, Tom, played by Man #1)

TOM: Waitress, another drink. I'm celebrating.

FRANKLIN: *(Mimes grabbing a drink. Suddenly drunk)* "Wine is constant proof that God loves us and loves to see us happy."

TOM: *(Whistles)* Take it off!

FRANKLIN: On the other hand, "Nothing is more like a fool than a drunken man." Oh, I know what you're thinking. I'm drunk too. You were expecting a merry old codger with twinkling eyes and you got this. Well, can you blame me? I've been hanging with Mr. Hedge Fund all evening.

TOM: *(Waving money)* Hey, let's get some service here.

FRANKLIN: How did I, one of the founding fathers, come to such a pass? … The founding fathers! Sounds so respectful. Truth is we were a bunch of hotheads. The only reason you don't know us today as criminals and traitors is because we won. Hotheads! But at least we believed in something besides money.

MAN #2: And now, the highlight of tonight's entertainment … Jenny!

FRANKLIN: Oh God! Another woman dancing in scanty attire. How many times have I … *(Jenny enters)* Um … We'll talk more later.

JENNY:
IT DOESN'T MATTER TO ME ONE JOT
IF YOU HAPPEN TO HAVE MONEY,
LOTS OF MONEY, OR NOT.
OUR MATCH WAS MADE IN HEAVEN ABOVE.
AND IT'S YOU, NOT YOUR FOURTEEN MILLION
IN A WELL-DIVERSIFIED PORTFOLIO I LOVE.

WHO CARES IF YOU'RE FLUSH WITH MONEY?
MY HEART IS PURE AND TRUE.
SO LET ME PUT YOUR MIND AT EASE.
I LOVE YOU BECAUSE YOU'RE YOU.

WE TWO HAVE SO MUCH IN COMMON.
THAT NO ONE CAN DENY.
YOU, AFTER ALL, HAVE THREE GOLDMINES,
AND SOON, DARLING, SO WILL I.

YOU'RE EVERYTHING A GIRL COULD WANT.
I DOTE ON EVERY TRAIT.
YOU'VE GOT REAL CLASS, REAL SAVOIR FAIRE,
REAL STYLE AND REAL ESTATE.

SO LET PEOPLE GAPE AND GOSSIP,
BECAUSE YOU'RE EIGHTY-TWO,
AND YOUR DOCTOR GIVES YOU
A YEAR TO LIVE.
I LOVE YOU BECAUSE YOU'RE YOU.

(Dance break. Dancing becomes more suggestive and more athletic)

AND WHO CARES IF YOUR DOCTOR TOLD YOU,
THERE ARE THINGS YOU SHOULDN'T DO?
SO WHAT IF OUR LOVE MAY PROVE TOO MUCH?
I'LL LOVE YOU – Oooh!
LOVE YOU - Ahh!
LOVE YOU – Mmm.
LOVE YOU- Oh!
LOVE YOU –
BECAUSE YOU'RE YOU.

(She looks down at the floor)

JENNY: Honey? You okay?

(Final beat of music. Tom claps and whistles)

TOM: Hey, that was hot!

FRANKLIN: (*Wiping his brow*) Was it? I didn't notice.

TOM: I mean it was like real dancing.

JENNY: (*Sarcastically*) Thanks. *(Starts to leave)*

TOM: Wait. Here's a tip for your performance. *(Points to Franklin)*

JENNY: A hundred bucks?

FRANKLIN: (*Cleaning steam off spectacles*) A fool and his money are soon parted.

TOM: Only … you have to have one drink with me.

JENNY: For that much, sure. What do you want?

TOM: Champagne. Best you got. *(She goes off-stage)*

FRANKLIN: He does not possess wealth. Wealth possesses him.

JENNY: *(Coming back with bottle)* Guess what I found? A bottle of Dom Perignon.

TOM: Perfect.

JENNY: *(Pouring)* So what are we celebrating?

TOM: My bonus for the year. One million dollars.

JENNY: A million dollars? What do you do, rob banks?

FRANKLIN: Close.

TOM: I'm a broker for a hedge fund.

JENNY: You run a fund to buy small trees?

TOM: No, you see …

JENNY: I know what a hedge fund is. I was joking.

TOM: Ah.

JENNY: When you dance half-naked for a living, it helps to have a sense of humor.

TOM: Among other things.

FRANKLIN: You know, Colonial women used to show
a lot of décolletage. Unless they lived in Massachusetts.
I remember Betsy Ross bending over her sewing.
I swear that's how the woman got three husbands.
Back then, we didn't use the word "hot" to describe
female beauty, but by any definition, Betsy was a hottie.

TOM: A million dollars sounds like a lot of money, I
guess.

FRANKLIN: Ten thousand Franklins.

TOM: The hell of it is, when you make that much,
you're expected to play your part to the hilt: designer
suits, 80-hour workweeks, a doorman apartment on
the Upper East Side. And then my wife has very
expensive tastes.

JENNY: Wow, you poor guy.

TOM: Sometimes, I just want to chuck the whole thing.

JENNY: So why aren't you celebrating your bonus with
your wife?

TOM: She's a fashion buyer for Bergdorf's. So she's
in Paris at the moment. Shopping.

JENNY: Ah. So you're shopping too.

TOM: Me? No, I'm just window shopping.   Tell me.
Are those real?

JENNY: Excuse me?

FRANKLIN: The heart of a fool is in his mouth.

TOM: I mean those cups definitely runneth over.

JENNY: What is it with you Wall Street guys?

TOM: Sorry, I was only trying to …

JENNY: You said one drink … *(Downs the rest)* I finished it.

TOM: Hey, there's no reason to …

JENNY: My tip.

TOM: What?

JENNY: You promised me a hundred dollar tip. I'd like it now

TOM: Fine. Here. Here's your tip. *(Shoves Franklin's head between her breasts)*

FRANKLIN: They're real.

JENNY: How dare you! *(Slaps him)*

TOM: Ow!

FRANKLIN: Experience keeps a dear school, but a fool …
Excuse me. I'm with her now. Which I must say I prefer.
(They exit)

TOM: Waitress, another drink. And a bag of ice.

(Lights fade)

SCENE 2: Jenny's Apartment

(There's a baby crying in the back room. Floyd, Jenny's boyfriend, played by Man #2, is reading a newspaper with trashy headline. So is Franklin)

FRANKLIN: They call this a newspaper. It's nothing but scandal, calamity and gossip. [*Reads latest ridiculous headline to us*] The trouble with being money is you can't move to Canada. My newspapers were much more entertaining … Oh, wait. Comics!

(Baby stops crying. Jenny enters)

JENNY: I think he's finally asleep.

FLOYD: That cryin' drives me crazy.

JENNY: It's not his fault. Doctor says he's colicky.

FRANKLIN: From the Latin "colicus" meaning colon. Do you mind if I help myself to more coffee?   After last night …

JENNY: Here. Here's something that should make you feel better.

FLOYD: A hundred dollar bill?

JENNY: Some Wall Street guy gave it to me.

FLOYD: For doin' what?

JENNY: For dancing and shaking my hips. What do you think I got it for?

FLOYD: You oughta quit that job.

JENNY: And what do we live on? Your unemployment insurance?

FRANKLIN: Ha! Ha! Ha! Sorry. Garfield makes me laugh. The cat, not the president. The president wasn't funny at all.

JENNY: I hate my job, Floyd. I didn't take 14 years of dance class to be an exotic dancer.   But it pays well, and we've got this baby to take care of now, so I guess I'll keep doing it for a while and sock away the money.

FLOYD: Yeah, well, what sort of man gives you a hundred dollars just to see you dance?

JENNY: A rich one, that's who. Said he'd just got a million dollars as a bonus.

FLOYD: A million bucks! And he's just throwin' it around, givin' it to anybody.

JENNY: Thanks, Floyd.

FLOYD: You know what I mean. If I had so much money, I didn't know what to do with it, I'd know what to do with it.

JENNY: Gee, wouldn't it be nice to be rich?

FLOYD: I'm glad you brought that up, Jenny. 'Cause I've got a plan. A plan to invest that money you made and turn it into somethin' big.

JENNY: Another plan?

FRANKLIN: By failing to plan, you are planning to fail.

FLOYD: Your hundred added to what I've saved up
just might be enough.

JENNY: Jesus, Floyd.

JENNY:
DO I HAVE TO REMIND YOU OF YOUR OTHER
GET RICH QUICK SCHEMES?
FLOYD:
WITH 20/20 HINDSIGHT,
IT'S SO EASY TO NITPICK SCHEMES.

JENNY:
THE INFLATABLE BOWLING BALL?
FLOYD:
BEFORE ITS TIME IS ALL.
JENNY:
EGGNOG-FLAVORED BEER?
FLOYD:
WOULD HAVE SOLD WELL ONCE A YEAR.
JENNY:
THE REFRIGERATOR CAM?
FLOYD:
SO YOU KNOW WHO TOOK THE HAM.
JENNY:
A FORMAL RUNNING SHOE?
FLOYD:
STAY IN SHAPE AND LOOK GOOD TOO.

OKAY, SOME OF THOSE IDEAS A' MINE
WEREN'T QUITE AS GOOD AS THIS.
BUT NOW I'VE DONE MY HOMEWORK,
AND THIS TIME I CAN'T MISS …

JENNY: All right. What's your plan this time?

FLOYD: Poker.

JENNY: Poker?

FRANKLIN: Poker?

FLOYD:
TEXAS HOLD-EM.
TEXAS HOLD-EM.
I KNOW A MAN WHO'D WIN
IF YOU BANKROLLED HIM.
I'M GONNA MAKE A FORTUNE.
YOU CAN COUNT ON ME.
CAUSE I'VE BECOME AN EXPERT
BY WATCHIN' ON TV.

TEXAS-HOLD EM.
TEXAS HOLD-EM.
I KNOW WHEN TO PLAY MY CARDS
AND WHEN TO FOLD 'EM.
DID I EVER MENTION
THAT LUCK'S MY MIDDLE NAME?
AND SOME DAY THEY WILL PUT ME
IN THE POKER HALL OF FAME.

FRANKLIN: And did I ever mention that diligence …
Wait! There's a Hall of Fame for Poker?

FLOYD:
WHEN IT COMES TO MAKIN' MONEY,
YOU GOTTA GO FOR BROKE.
LET THE SUCKERS SAVE UP SLOWLY.
WITH THEIR THREE PER CENT CDS.
AND THEIR SIXTY-HOUR WORK WEEKS,
AND THEIR FIXED ANNUITIES.

LET THEM STRUGGLE TO SURVIVE
AND RETIRE AT SIXTY-FIVE.
I CAN MAKE OUR FORTUNE IN ONE STROKE.

FRANKLIN: We are all born ignorant, but one must work hard to remain stupid.

TEXAS HOLD-EM.
TEXAS HOLD-EM.
THE CARDS HAVE ALWAYS DONE
JUST WHAT I TOLD EM.
I GRANT YOU IN THE PAST
I CAUGHT A FEW BAD BREAKS.
AND MAYBE ONCE OR TWICE
I MADE SOME SMALL MISTAKES.

JENNY: Small?

FLOYD:
BUT THIS TIME WILL BE DIFFERENT
CAUSE I'VE GOT WHAT IT TAKES.
TEXAS …

JENNY: Hold it! *(Music stops abruptly)* I'm not giving you the money.

FLOYD: Trust me.   I know what I'm doin'.

FRANKLIN: That's exactly what John Adams said to me in Paris, just before he offended the entire French Court. Adams' idea of diplomacy was a direct insult followed by a petulant whine.

JENNY: A hundred dollars? That's a week's worth of groceries.

(We hear baby crying on the monitor)

JENNY: Oh God, the baby again. I'll be right back.

(She leaves the room. Floyd looks at Franklin hesitantly. Franklin feels him staring)

FRANKLIN: *(To Floyd, backing up)* When in doubt, don't.

FLOYD: Honey, you're gonna thank me for this someday. *(Grabs Franklin)* Look, this is just a loan. I'm gonna mark this bill with your name in the corner, so I remember to return it. *(Starts writing on Franklin's hand)*

FRANKLIN: It takes many good deeds to build a reputation. And only one bad one to lose it.   You know it's a federal crime to … *(Looks at his hand)* Jenny, how sweet.

FLOYD:
THERE'S A TOURNAMENT IN VEGAS,
FREE AIRFARE AND HOTEL.
SO I'LL USE ALL OUR MONEY
FOR THE ONE THING I KNOW WELL:

TEXAS HOLD-EM.
FRANKLIN:
TEXAS HOLD-EM.
FLOYD:
TEXAS HOLD-EM.
FRANKLIN:
TEXAS HOLD-EM.
HE BELIEVES THAT BILL OF GOODS
LAS VEGAS SOLD HIM.

FLOYD:
NO, YOU CANNOT PLAY IT TIMID,
WHEN YOU'RE HEARIN' FORTUNE'S CALL.
FRANKLIN:
AS THEY SAY IN PROVERBS,
PRIDE GOES BEFORE THE FALL.
FLOYD:
YEAH, YOU GOTTA BE ALL IN.
THAT'S HOW YOU WIN
FRANKLIN:
OR LOSE
BOTH:
IT ALL.
FRANKLIN:
Sin City, here we come!
BOTH:
TEXAS HOLD-EM.

(Floyd grabs Franklin and heads out door.)

SCENE 3: Las Vegas Casino *(Sports announcer, played by Man #1, enters)*

SPORTS ANNCR: Ladies and gentlemen, welcome to the World Series ...of Poker. This is Ernie LaCoste reporting live from Las Vegas. But first, this word from our sponsor.

(Franklin and Floyd enter)

FRANKLIN: It's not too late to change your mind, Floyd. I have a very bad feeling about this. It's not that I dislike games. I myself was an avid chess player. I even wrote an essay called *The Morals of Chess*, which is a classic of its kind. Perhaps you've read it? No, I suppose not. My point is chess is about intelligence and skill, whereas this ...

ERNIE: Welcome back. And now let's meet our first two contestants: Millionaire socialite, Brooke Fairbanks, and unemployed machinist, Floyd Buckwaller. Brooke, are you ready for this match?

BROOKE: Oh, I hope so. I've been practicing my poker face for weeks. Look! *(Passes hand in front of face)* Can you tell what I'm thinking?

ERNIE: No, you look completely blank.

BROOKE: Well, you try.

ERNIE: How about you, Floyd? Are you ready to go up against Brooke?

FLOYD: Am I ever!

FRANKLIN: I don't know. There's something about this woman that doesn't ring true. If I were you ...

FLOYD: Let's get started!

FRANKLIN: Where sense is wanting, everything is wanting.

ERNIE: All right. Let's begin. *(Starts dealing)*

BROOKE:
I KNOW WHAT OTHER PEOPLE SAY.
DUMB BLONDE.
GET A LOAD OF HER. HEY, HEY.
DUMB BLONDE.
THEY DON'T SEE ANY WAY
I CAN DO AS WELL AS THEY,
CAUSE EVERY TIME I PLAY, I PLAY
DUMB BLONDE.

ERNIE: Brooke?

BROOKE: Gosh, I don't know.

BROOKE:
FROM THE MOMENT I SIT DOWN.
DUMB BLONDE.
IN A TIGHT, REVEALING GOWN.
DUMB BLONDE.
I USE THIS LITTLE VOICE
AND TALK BREATHILY BY CHOICE.
MY OPPONENTS ALL REJOICE. Yay!
DUMB BLOND.

ERNIE: Brooke. Still waiting.

BROOKE: I guess fifty.

ERNIE: Actually, that's worth a hundred.

BROOKE: Is it?

FLOYD: Call.

FLOYD:
DUM, DUM, DUM, DUM …

(Continuous. Becomes doo-wop number)

BROOKE:
THEY DON'T SEE THE WAY I ACT
IS JUST A CLEVER CON.
SO THEY GET OVERCONFIDENT.
AND SOON – Oops! - THEIR MONEYS GONE.
SO IN SUM, WHO'S REALLY DUMB?

BROOKE: Another one of these white chips.

FRANKLIN: *(To Floyd)* Please. Don't do it.

FLOYD: Call.

BOTH:
DUM, DUM, DUM, DUM … *(Continuous)*

BROOKE:
I REALLY HAVE A PHD I EARNED AT MIT,
WHICH HELPS ME CALCULATE THE ODDS.
RIGHT NOW … At 3.67 to 1 … THEY FAVOR ME.
AND MY IQ.
BOTH:
NOT A CLUE, NOT A CLUE.
BROOKE:
162–OOH-OOH-OOH.

BROOKE: I check.

FLOYD: Is that right? Well …

FRANKLIN: Believe me, you really want to check.

FLOYD: I'll bet a hundred.

BROOKE: Oh dear.

FRANKLIN: Oh dear.

BROOKE: Well, I guess I'll match that. And raise you two hundred.

FLOYD: Call. Full house. *(Lays down his cards)*

BROOKE: Oh, my. I just have a lot of little red hearts.

FLOYD*: (Starts to take pot)* Well, better luck …

BROOKE: A three, a four, a five, a six … *(voice suddenly smarter)* … and a seven.

ERNIE: Straight flush.

FLOYD: What?

ERNIE: Game and match to the lady!

BROOKE: Goodness. Lucky me. *(Starts gathering in chips)*

FRANKLIN: A fool and his money … Or did I say that one already? Fools make feasts and wise men eat them.

A Fool and His Money...

<u>FRANKLIN</u>:
DUM, DUM, DUM, DUM, DUM. (*Continues*)
<u>ERNIE</u>:
DUM, DUM. DUM, DUM, DUM. (*Continues*)
<u>FLOYD</u>:
DUM, DUM, DUM, DUM, DUM. (*Continues*)

<u>BROOKE</u>:
THEN I FLASH MY BRIGHTEST SMILE,
DUMB BLONDE.

WHICH BLINDS THEM TO MY INNER GUILE,
DUMB BLONDE.

I PLAY OUT MY PART
EVEN AS I BREAK THEIR HEART.
CAUSE NOBODY'S AS SMART AS A SMART ...

FRANKLIN:
DUM.
ERNIE:
DUM.
FLOYD:
DUM
BROOKE:
DUM.
ALL:
DUM!

BROOKE:
DUMB BLONDE!

(Blackout)

SCENE 4: Front Yard of LA Mansion

(We see bush shaped like elephant, played by Man #2. Brooke enters with Franklin. Franklin is wearing sunglasses, has a sun reflector and a lawn chair)

BROOKE: Jorge! Jorge!   *(Hispanic gardener, played by Man #1, enters)*

JORGE: Yes, Mrs. Fairbanks.

BROOKE: You have to fix this bush.

JORGE: What's wrong with it?

BROOKE: What's wrong is it looks like an elephant.

JORGE: That's because you asked me to shape it like an elephant.

BROOKE: Yes, I know. But my husband doesn't like it.

JORGE: I did my best.

BROOKE: No, no, it looks fine. It's just that an elephant is a symbol of the Republican party. And my husband doesn't want anyone to think we're Republicans.

JORGE: You are not?

BROOKE: Of course we are. But in LA you have to be seen as ultra-liberal. And we don't want our wacko celebrity neighbors getting their designer knickers into a twist. Can you turn it into a donkey?

JORGE: I can try.

FRANKLIN: They want a symbol to tell their neighbors who they are and they choose an ass. Did they really think this through?

BROOKE: Jorge, have I paid you recently?

JORGE: You gave me a check last week.

FRANKLIN: If you want a real symbol of America, I suggest the turkey, a true Native American and a bird of courage.

BROOKE: Well then here. *(Points to Franklin)*

JORGE: What's this?

BROOKE: A small bonus. I was lucky at cards.

FRANKLIN: I wanted the turkey to be our national symbol, but I was overruled, and for what? The bald eagle, a bird of bad moral character, who preys on the weak and steals from the helpless.

JORGE: Thank you, Mrs. Fairbanks.

BROOKE: Please, call me Brooke. *(Puts her hand on his arm)*

FRANKLIN: *(Noticing)* Though perhaps those who voted for the eagle had a clearer notion of America's future than I did.

BROOKE: Just out of curiosity, what will you do with the money?

JORGE: I will buy another weedwhacker.

BROOKE: A weedwhacker? You wild and crazy man.

JORGE: Someday, I will buy a second leafblower, and then a second lawnmower, and a second truck, which my son will drive. And then, who knows, perhaps a whole fleet of trucks.

FRANKLIN: Work as if you will live for a hundred years. Pray as if you will die tomorrow.

BROOKE: Well, aren't you the man with the plan.
I used to work for a living. I taught calculus to college freshmen. What a waste of time.

JORGE: I would have thought teaching would be … rewarding.

BROOKE: Well, then you'd be wrong. The pay was terrible and most of the students didn't want to be there. So I married a rich man, and now I play…I play house, I play cards, I play dumb, I play around.

FRANKLIN: It is the working man who is happy. It is the idle man who is … (*Realizes what he's saying, jumps up*) … miserable.

(*He starts doing calisthenics*)

BROOKE: Would you like to come in for a drink? A margarita, perhaps.

JORGE: It's a little early for that.

BROOKE: I just thought … It's awfully hot out here.

JORGE: I'm used to it.

BROOKE: It's all right. My husband is away on business. He's always away on business.

FRANKLIN: Some people die at 25 and aren't buried until 75.

BROOKE: Do you ever watch soap operas, Jorge?

JORGE: No, ma'am. I don't have the time.

FRANKLIN: Time is money.

BROOKE: Too bad. Some of them are quite entertaining.

FRANKLIN: Course in my day, we didn't have soap operas. We were lucky to have soap. I used to take something called an air bath. You stand naked in front of an open window and allow the breeze to cool and freshen you. It was our own form of television.

BROOKE: Anyway, in these soap operas, married women are always finding themselves in … predicaments. Have you ever found yourself in a predicament, Jorge?

JORGE: I find myself in one now. A very thorny one.

BROOKE: What?

JORGE: The bush.

BROOKE: Oh, right. Another time, then. *(She exits)*

(Jorge watches her leave and shakes his head)

~ **Ben** was a big believer in air baths ~

JORGE:
YOU DON'T EVEN KNOW WHAT YOU HAVE,
DO YOU?
YOU DON'T EVEN UNDERSTAND.
EVERYTHING I'M SLAVING FOR,
SAVING FOR, CRAVING FOR
IS ALREADY THERE
IN YOUR SOFT, UNCALLOUSED HAND.

JORGE: A donkey ... *(Takes out notepad and pen and starts to sketch)*

FRANKLIN: You know, Jorge, you and I have a lot in common. My father came here from England to make a better life for his family. I had to quit school at ten to help him in his trade as a candlemaker. I hated it. Wanted to run away to sea. Then at twelve, I was apprenticed to a printer, and being around all those books changed my life. So, you see, we're not all that different.

(Jorge starts cutting the bush referring to his sketch)

JORGE:
I'M CHASING A DREAM,
THE AMERICAN DREAM.
ACROSS A GREAT DIVIDE.
I'M CROSSING A STREAM
ON THE BACK OF A DREAM
TRYING TO REACH THE OTHER SIDE.

(Franklin joins in)

BOTH:
I'M CHASING A DREAM,
THE AMERICAN DREAM.
JORGE:
BUT IS IT WORTH THE COST?
WHEN THE PEOPLE WHO ALREADY
HAVE THE DREAM
ALWAYS LOOK SO LOST.

JORGE:
I'M CHASING A DREAM,
TRYING TO CATCH IT,
TRYING TO GRAB THE TAIL.
TRYING TO NAB THIS MODERN, UNHOLY GRAIL.

BOTH:
THOUGH MOST OF THE PEOPLE
WHO CHASE THIS DREAM WILL FAIL.

BOTH:
I'M CHASING A DREAM,
AND NO MATTER HOW TIRED
OR DOUBTFUL I MAY BE,
I'LL NEVER WALK AWAY FROM THIS DREAM,
CAUSE THE DREAM'S NOT JUST FOR ME.

(Young Hispanic girl, Jorge's daughter, appears on the other side of the stage playing guitar)

JUANITA:
I'M CHASING A DREAM.
THE AMERICAN DREAM.
THE ONE THAT'S ON TV.
AND AM I TO BLAME
IF IT ISN'T THE SAME
AS THE DREAM MY PARENTS WANT FOR ME?

I'M CHASING A DREAM,
BUT IT'S MORE THAN A DREAM
WHEN EVERYTHING I DO,
EVERY STEP THAT I TAKE
FROM THE MOMENT I WAKE
IS TO MAKE THE DREAM COME TRUE.

ALL 3:
I'M CHASING A DREAM,
THERE IN THE DISTANCE,
SHIMMERING LIKE A STAR.
JUANITA:
HIGH IN THE SKY,
THAT'S WHERE THE BEST DREAMS ARE.

THE 2 MEN:
THOUGH MOST OF THE PEOPLE
WILL NEVER REACH THAT FAR.
JUANITA:
IF I REALLY WANT THE DREAM, I'LL GO FAR.

ALL 3:
I'M CHASING A DREAM,
THE AMERICAN DREAM.
JUANITA:
WHY SHOULDN'T I DREAM TOO?
ALL 3:
BUT WHY DOES IT SEEM,
THAT NOW EVERY DREAM,
MUST HAVE MONEY TO MAKE IT COME TRUE?

ALL 3:
I'M CHASING THE DREAM,
THE AMERICAN DREAM.
JUANITA:
I'LL PROVE WHAT I CAN BE.

JORGE:
BUT SOMETIMES I THINK THE TRUTH IS,
THE DREAM IS CHASING ME.

(Jorge finishes with the plant and walks into the scene with Juanita)

JUANITA:
MAYBE I'LL FIND THE TRUTH IS,
THAT DREAMS ARE DESTINY.

(She starts writing down the last line on a piece of paper)

FRANKLIN: *(To us)* Now this is what I'm talking about. This is why America was founded. So people can pursue their dreams in peace and harmony.

JORGE: You sing so beautiful.

JUANITA: Thank you, father.

JORGE: But don't you have homework?

JUANITA: I finished it. I always do it first, so I can sing without guilt.

JORGE: Why would you feel guilt?

JUANITA: Because I know what my finishing college means to you.

FRANKLIN: You see? Harmony … mostly.

JORGE: It should mean something to you too.

JUANITA: Oh, it does. It means that I will get a good job and work hard to provide a good life for my children, so that they can go to college and get a good job and work hard to provide a good life for their children, et cetera, et cetera, et cetera.

FRANKLIN: Of course, parents and children will always have different dreams. But if they talk things out sensibly …

JORGE: What do you mean, et cetera, et cetera?

JUANITA: It's a word they teach you in school that means boring.

FRANKLIN: Oh dear.

JORGE: That's not fair, Juanita! I only want what's best for you.

JUANITA: I know you do, father.   But maybe I'm not meant for college.

FRANKLIN: She has a point, Jorge. Not everyone ...

JORGE: Do you want to end up like your sister? Living in poverty with that loser.

JUANITA: He's not a loser. He's an artist.

JORGE: Oh, please. He sits around all day pretending to paint while your sister waits tables and gives him her tip money. Is that what you want for yourself?

JUANITA: Maybe he'll make money someday, maybe he won't, but at least he's painting more than houses!

FRANKLIN: Okay, maybe they're not the best example.

JUANITA: I'm sorry. That was unfair.

FRANKLIN: Whatever's begun in anger ends in shame.

JUANITA: ... I'd better start dinner.

JORGE: *(Softening)* You think you can make a living as a singer?

JUANITA: I hope to someday.

FRANKLIN: *(To Jorge)* He who lives on hope will die fasting.

JORGE: Wait. I have a present for you. *(Gives her Franklin)*

JUANITA: What's this?

JORGE: To record one of your songs. To make, what you call it, a demo, so the world can hear what I hear.

FRANKLIN: There you see. This is also what America is about. Sacrificing for a dream.

JUANITA: No, father. You need that money for your business.

JORGE: I will grow old pursuing my dream. You should try for yours while you're young. Only make me one promise.

JUANITA: What?

JORGE: Don't tell your mother where you got the money.

JUANITA: Thank you, padre mio. Thank you.

FRANKLIN: Hide not your talents. They for use were made. What's a sundial in the shade?

SCENE 5. A Recording Studio

(Juanita, carrying her guitar, enters with Franklin. Jake, played by Man #2, is eating lunch)

JUANITA: Excuse me. Anyone here?

JAKE: Yes, can I help you?

JUANITA: Hi. I'd like to use your studio to record a song.

JAKE: Great.   How many hours would you like?

JUANITA: I don't know. How much does it cost?

JAKE: One fifty an hour.

JUANITA: Oh. Could I get a half hour?

JAKE: Sorry. We always round up to the nearest hour. Besides, it takes time to get the right take.   Then you have to adjust the pitch, get rid of breaths, balance the sound …

JUANITA: It doesn't have to be perfect, and I don't care if people know that I breathe. One or two takes is all I need.

JAKE: All right. Come back at 3.

JUANITA: I have class at 3.

JAKE: Well, right now my engineer's at lunch.

JUANITA: Oh, I see.

FRANKLIN: *(To Juanita)* Energy and persistence conquer all things.

JUANITA: I don't suppose you could act as engineer.

JAKE: Me?

FRANKLIN: Constant dropping wears away stones.

JUANITA: It would mean a lot.

FRANKLIN: Little strokes fell great oaks.

JUANITA: It won't take more than ten minutes.

FRANKLIN: To succeed, jump as quickly at opportunities as you do at conclusions.

JUANITA: I would be so grateful.

JAKE: All right. What the hell? I'm Jake.

JUANITA: Juanita.

JAKE: Take me a few second to set you up. You ever recorded before?

JUANITA: No.

JAKE: Most people first time, they overenunciate. Worst thing you can do. Try not to hit the consonants or you'll get a pop.

JUANITA: No pop.

JAKE: And since it's all audio, you really have to act with your voice. If you don't, the song won't have any conviction.

JUANITA: Conviction. Got it.

FRANKLIN: The art of acting consists in keeping people from coughing.

JAKE: We'll set one mic for you, and one for your guitar. *(He starts doing so)* That way we can control the balance.

FRANKLIN: *(Seeing other instruments)* You know, I used to play the guitar. As well as the violin, the viola da gamba and the harp. Would you mind if I played along? *(He picks up a second guitar)* An "electric" guitar? I guess we know who to thank for that, don't we?

JAKE: All right. I'll be behind the glass. I'll give a signal when to start. *(He leaves. We hear his voice from the speakers)* The lovely and stubborn Juanita, take one.

(She laughs)

FRANKLIN: She laughs at everything you say. Why? Because she has fine teeth. Hold on. Let me just check the sound. *(Shreds the guitar with fast picking and heavy metal effects)* Like riding a bicycle. *(To Juanita)* Okay. When you're ready.

JUANITA:
I WASN'T THE BEST CHILD.
SOMETIMES I'D TELL A LIE.
I DROVE MY TEACHER'S WILD
I MADE MY MOTHER CRY.

I NEVER GAVE MUCH HEED
WHEN FRIENDS WOULD GIVE ADVICE.
I NEVER SAW THEIR NEED,
I GUESS I PAID A PRICE.

(Franklin starts to accompany her)

JUANITA:
MY LIFE WAS TWISTING, STALLING
I FELT LIKE I WAS FALLING
INTO AN ENDLESS SKY.
TELL ME HOW WAS I TO KNOW
WHERE ALL OF THIS WOULD GO?
HOW DID I FALL SO HIGH?

I NEVER HAD A CLUE
OF WHAT IT MEANS TO LIVE.
AND SO I NEVER KNEW
YOU GET MORE WHEN YOU GIVE.

WHEN I LOOK BACK TODAY
ON WHERE I'VE BEEN I KNOW
I'VE COME A LONG, LONG WAY
BUT I HAD SO FAR TO GO.

NO, I DON'T MIND CONFESSING,
I DON'T DESERVE THIS BLESSING.
SO CAN YOU TELL ME WHY:
WHY AM I STANDING HERE WITH YOU?
WHAT GOOD DEED DID I DO?
HOW DID I FALL SO HIGH?

EVERY DAY,
THAT'S MY TASK.
WHEN I PRAY
I WILL ASK.

HOW DID SUCH IMPERFECTION
LEAD ME IN THIS DIRECTION?
CAN YOU TELL ME WHY:
WHY AM I STANDING HERE WITH YOU?
AFTER ALL THAT I'VE BEEN THROUGH,
HOW DID I FALL,
HOW DID I FALL SO HIGH?

(Jake walks into recording room)

JAKE: Is this a joke? Did one of my friends put you up to this?

JUANITA: I'm sorry?

JAKE: Where did you learn to sing like that?

JUANITA: Listening to others.   Didn't it sound good?

JAKE: It sounded fantastic! Did you write that?

JUANITA: Yes.

FRANKLIN: I wrote countless songs in my day.
Simple and sincere is always best.

JAKE: And to think I almost threw you out.

FRANKLIN: I once wrote a song called "My Plain
Country Joan," that extolled the virtues of my wife,
Deborah.   For some reason, she never took to the
song.

JAKE: You know, we could enhance this a little.
I could bring in a few friends. We could make this
demo a gem. (*Starts dialing on cell phone*)

FRANKLIN: More instruments? Good idea! This time,
I could play the harp.

JUANITA: I only have the hundred.

FRANKLIN: Or the glass harmonica. I invented that, you
know. Mozart and Beethoven composed for it.

JAKE: Keep the money. I'll do it for free.

JUANITA: What? Why?

JAKE: Consider it an investment. You can pay me
back when you're rich and famous.

FRANKLIN: You don't happen to have a glass harmonica here in the studio, do you?

JUANITA: What makes you think I'll be rich and famous?

JAKE: I know talent when I hear it.

FRANKLIN: In this world, nothing is certain except death. It used to be death and taxes, but I had to change that one.

JAKE: *(Into phone)* Colin, this is Jake. I need you to do me a favor. *(Lights fade)*

SCENE 6: Street Outside with Bus Stop

JUANITA: *(Talking into cell phone)* Padre mio. I
did it! I recorded the demo. It took me three hours.

FRANKLIN: It's a wonderful recording, Jorge. Even without
the glass harmonica.

JUANITA: Yes, yes, I missed my class, but wait till you hear.
I am bringing it home to play for you.

(A thief, played by Man #1, enters)

THIEF: Gimme your purse.

JUANITA: What? No!

THIEF: Girl, don't make me hurt you.

FRANKLIN: *(To Juanita)* Hear reason or she will make
you feel her.

JUANITA: I am not giving this up.

THIEF: I'm warning you.

JUANITA: NO!

FRANKLIN: When passion drives you, let reason hold
the reins!

*(Thief grabs purse and Franklin. Juanita grabs hold
of Franklin's other arm. Brief tug of war. Jake runs on)*

JAKE: You! Drop the purse!

THIEF: Says who? *(Grabs him by the lapels)*

JUANITA: Aiyah! *(Spins and executes a high kick that stuns thief)* Huhn! *(Stamps on his foot, causing him to slump to the ground in pain. Then stands over him in fighting pose, jerking one fist forward and one back. She repeats this three times in rapid succession, breathing out forcefully each time, then stands ready to strike again)*

THIEF: Holy crap! *(He runs off)*

JAKE: Holy crap!

FRANKLIN: Holy cravat!

(She breathes out slowly and relaxes arms)

JUANITA: Are you all right?

FRANKLIN: No, my arms are … oh, him.

JAKE: I'm fine. You know karate?

JUANITA: I'm taking a self-defense class in college. Who knew it would actually work?

JAKE: One class?! Good thing I agreed to do the demo.

JUANITA: Good thing. But how …

JAKE: I was watching out the window when you left.
You waiting for a bus?

JUANITA: Yes.

JAKE: My car's around the corner. Let me take you home.

JUANITA: It's a long drive.

FRANKLIN: He that can have patience can have what he will.

JAKE: I don't mind.

FRANKLIN: In fact, genius is nothing but a greater aptitude for patience.

JUANITA: Why are you so nice to me?

JAKE: I assure you, my motives are totally selfish. Can I see you again?

JUANITA: You don't waste time, do you?

FRANKLIN: Do you love life? Then do not squander time, for that's the stuff life is made of.

JAKE: Can't afford to. Once you're rich and famous, you'll forget I exist.

JUANITA: You think that little of me?

JAKE: No, I think that much of you.

FRANKLIN: *(To Juanita)* Search others for their virtues, thyself for thy vices.

JUANITA: You should be paid for what you've done. Take the money, please.

JAKE: All right. I'll take it, if you let me use it to buy you dinner tonight.

JUANITA: Tonight?

JAKE: Don't think of it as a date. More like a celebration between two business partners.

JUANITA: I have homework.

JAKE: I won't keep you out late. I have a friend who runs a nice Italian restaurant. What do you say?

FRANKLIN: "I saw few die of hunger. Of eating, a hundred thousand." Though how that applies here, I really can't say. "Hunger is the best pickle." No, that doesn't work either.

JUANITA: I say … yes.

SCENE 7: Italian Restaurant

(Italian owner, Luigi, played by Man #1, enters)

LUIGI:
WELCOME TO LUIGI'S, MY FRIEND.
IF YOU'VE NEVER BEEN BEFORE,
YOU'RE IN FOR QUITE A TREAT.
IT'S THE PLACE TO WINE AND DINE
AND SPEND … A LOVELY TIME
WRAPPED UP IN WHAT YOU EAT.

(Lights reveal Jake and Juanita dining and clearly enjoying their date)

COME TO LUIGI'S
ORDER SOME PASTA.
SO MOLTO BENE,
I MAKE JUST FOR YOU.
HERE AT LUIGI'S
FOOD IS MY PASSION.
I MAKE IT YOUR PASSION TOO.

OUR PARMIGIANA
IS CELEBRATED
THE GLITTERATI
COME THROUGH OUR DOORS.
PEOPLE FROM EUROPE
FLY HERE TO DINE HERE.
FOOD IS MY PASSION.
I BET IT'S YOURS.

ALL DAY YOU MAKE MONEY,
BUT WHAT GOOD IS MONEY?
IT WON'T MAKE YOU HAPPY.
IT WON'T LIFT YOUR MOOD.

BUT DINE AT LUIGI'S,
OH BOYA SUCH GIOIA,
THAT'S WHY YOU MAKE MONEY:
TO PAY FOR MY FOOD.
WHY ELSE YOU MAKE MONEY
BUT TO ENJOY FOOD?

YOU MARRY A WOMAN.
SHE MAY MAKE YOU HAPPY,
BUT SHE'S A THE SAME WOMAN
NIGHT AFTER NIGHT.
BUT EACH TIME YOU COME HERE,
YOU TRY SOMETHING DIFFERENT,
THERE'S SOMETHING TO SATISFY
EACH APPETITE.

WHEN YOU WANT TO CELEBRATE,
LUIGI'S IS THE PLACE.
AND WHEN YOU FEEL SAD,
IT HELPS TO FEED YOUR FACE.

FEED A FEVER, FEED A COLD,
AND YOU'LL SOON FEEL GOOD AS GOLD.
FEED ARTHRITIS, SCHIZOPHRENIA.
LARYNGITIS, NYMPHOMANIA.

We have oysters!

FOOD IS THE ONE TRUE PANACEA.
AND THE FOOD YOU GET HERE: MAMA MIA!

(Luigi walks over to Jake and Juanita's table)

LUIGI: Ah, Jake, my friend. How was your meal?

JAKE: Perfetto.

FRANKLIN: Si, molto bene. I have a weakness for anything smothered in Parmesan cheese.

JAKE: And thanks for the free gelati.

LUIGI: He's a good fellow, this Jake.

JUANITA: Is he? *(Teasing)* I haven't quite made up my mind.

FRANKLIN: *(To Juanita)* Be slow in choosing a friend, slower in changing. Though in this case, I have to agree with Luigi.

LUIGI: Maybe I see you again, eh? Tuesday's a pasta night. I give you a quiet table in the back.

JAKE: Geez, Luigi. We just met ... That is, unless ... you want to have dinner again?

JUANITA: Tuesday? I do happen to be free that night.

FRANKLIN: Great! I'm free then too.

JAKE: Well, see you Tuesday. Here. (*Gives him Franklin*) The change goes to our waitress.

FRANKLIN: Oh. Oh yes. I forgot I was paying for the meal.

LUIGI: You always tip so nice. Ciao, my friend.

J&J: Ciao. *(They exit)*

FRANKLIN: Ciao. I'm going to miss those two.

LUIGI:
AT FIRST OUR MENU
IT MAY LOOK PRICEY
TRY IT AND THEN YOU
MOAN WITH DELIGHT.
THE FOOD IS SO TASTY, SO JUICY, SO SPICY.
YOU SEE THAT THE PRICEY IS RIGHT.

FOOD IS LIFE'S GREAT PLEASURE,
I SHOULD KNOW SO.
AND THE DINNERS HERE?
DELIZIOSO!

FRANKLIN: Beware the hobby that eats. To lengthen
thy life, lessen thy meals. Eat to live. Don't … (*Luigi
crams slice of bread in Franklin's mouth to shut him up*)
Mmm. Garlic!

LUIGI:
SO COME TO LUIGI'S
PASTA OR POLLO
PESCI, BISTECCA,
THERE'S SO MUCH TO CHOOSE.
COME TO LUIGI'S
FOOD IS MY PASSION.
IT'S THE ONE PASSION
YOU NEVER LOSE.

More?

(Policeman, played by Man #2, enters)

POLICE: Hey, Luigi, how's business?

LUIGI: Officer Gaines, how nice to see you. Would you like some dinner? On the house, of course.

POLICE: Not tonight. I got plans. Any problems with the cars in the lot recently.

LUIGI: No, that all seems to have stopped since you offered your "protection."

POLICE: Well, good. Glad I could help.

LUIGI: And in return, I hope you will accept the usual fee.

(Gives him Franklin)

POLICE: I wouldn't call it a fee, Luigi. I'd call it a small show of gratitude.

LUIGI: Thank you for allowing me to express my gratitude four times a month.

FRANKLIN: He that is of the opinion money will do everything may well be suspected of doing everything for money.

LUIGI: Have a good night, Officer Gaines.

POLICE: Oh, I intend to.

SCENE 8: Street

*(Music to "The World Runs on Money" starts up.
Hooker enters)*

HOOKER: Hey, baby. Lookin' for a good time? Oh,
you're a cop.

POLICE: Relax. I'm here to do some business.

HOOKER: Ain't that a wedding ring on your finger?

POLICE: What if it is?

FRANKLIN: *(To Hooker)* Where there's marriage
without love, there will be love without marriage.

HOOKER: Well, if you got the bread, I got the spread.

FRANKLIN: My point exactly.

*(Franklin raps to a montage of scenes: policeman gives
money to hooker, who then gives money to drug dealer, who
gives money to female lawyer who gives money to judge who
gives it to his mistress, a nun, who gives it to her daughter to
buy a gun. The gun owner gives it to a female lobbyist who
gives it to a politician who then votes thumbs down on a bill)*

FRANKLIN:
I FEEL DIRTY, I FEEL FILTHY,
I FEEL CHEAP AND I FEEL LOW.
TAKE THE MONEY, HERE'S THE MONEY.
I'VE GOT MONEY, SO LET'S GO.
IN THE BOARDROOM, IN THE BACKROOM,
IN THE BEDROOM, THEY WANT DOUGH.

LET'S BE HONEST, HONEY,
THE WORLD RUNS ON MONEY.

OTHER 3:
IT TAKES MONEY.
OOH-OOH-OHH.
IT TAKES MONEY.
OOH-OOH-OHH.

FRANKLIN:
FROM THE HOOKER TO THE DEALER
WHO SELLS UPPERS BY THE DIME,
TO THE LAWYER WHO DEFENDS HIM
FOR THE 27TH TIME,
TO A JUDGE WHO KNOWS A THING OR TWO
ABOUT A LIFE OF CRIME.

JUDGE: We find the defendant guilty. *(Takes money from lawyer)* But hey, no one's perfect. *(Drug dealer is set free)*

FRANKLIN:
DON'T YOU FIND IT FUNNY?
THE WORLD RUNS ON MONEY.

OTHER 3:
IT TAKES MONEY.
OOH-OOH-OHH.
IT TAKES MONEY.
OOH-OOH-OHH.

FRANKLIN:
FROM HIS HONOR WITH NO HONOR,
TO HIS MISTRESS, WHO'S A NUN,
TO HER DAUGHTER, WHO'S AN EX-MARINE
AND WANTS TO BUY A GUN.

AND THOUGH SHE HAS TRAUMATIC STRESS,
A GUN SHOW SELLS HER ONE.

MAN: I'll need to see some ID.

WOMAN: To buy a gun?

MAN: God, no. To write a check.

WOMAN: I'll pay cash.

FRANKLIN:
LEARN YOUR LESSON, SONNY.
THE WORLD RUNS ON MONEY.

OTHER 3:
IT TAKES MONEY.
OOH-OOH-OHH.
IT TAKES MONEY.
OOH-OOH-OHH.

FRANKLIN:
THEN THE GUN PURVEYORS DONATE MONEY
TO THE NRA,
TO ELECT A GUTLESS CONGRESS
WHO'LL DO EVERYTHING THEY SAY.
NEVER MIND HOW MANY CHILDREN
IN THE WORLD GET BLOWN AWAY.

Justice will not be served until those who are unaffected
are as outraged as those who are.

PERHAPS IT'S NOT SO FUNNY,
THE WORLD RUNS ON …

(Music cuts-off)

Scene 9: Hotel Room

(Politician, played by Man #1, and female lobbyist enter. She uses the phone)

WOMAN: Room Service? Would you send up champagne to room 117? Congressman Cheezly and I are celebrating our victory.

FRANKLIN: Laws without morals are in vain. Only a virtuous people are capable of freedom.

MAN: I wish you hadn't mentioned my name.

WOMAN: Relax. If they told the press about every politician who had an affair here, this hotel would be out of business.

MAN: Yes, but every politician isn't sleeping with one of his lobbyists.

FRANKLIN: Politicians are a lot like diapers. They should be changed frequently and for the same reasons.

WOMAN: Darling, you did a great service to your country today: defending the second amendment.

MAN: I did. Didn't I?

FRANKLIN: The second amendment. That's the one amendment where I wish we'd been a little more specific. If we'd said the right to bear muskets …

WOMAN: I was very proud of you. *(They kiss)*

"It's the Right to <u>Bear</u> <u>Arms</u>, not the Right to <u>Arm</u> <u>Bea</u>...hey, are listening to me?!"

FRANKLIN: Course the Constitutional Convention itself was a mess. Of the supposed 74 delegates, 19 never made it, only 30 stayed the whole time, New Hampshire showed up two months late, New York left early and Rhode Island never showed up at all.   And this is the document constructionists parse with such reverence. Truth is, it was a slapdash effort.

WOMAN: Mind if I use this bill for a straw?

(She starts preparing a line of cocaine)

FRANKLIN: Words may show a man's wit, but actions …
Wait! You're planning to use me, one of the Founding
Fathers, as a delivery mechanism for an illicit drug?!
You know, George would be a better choice. He and Martha
took snuff all the time. He even laced his snuff with brandy.
I'm sure he'd be more than happy to help you out. *(Speaking
into woman's purse)*. George, I know you're in there. Don't
be bashful. *(Woman mimes rolling him into a straw by
spinning him around)*. Oh dear, I'm getting dizzy. I must say,
I have been in this world since January 17th, seventeen aught
six, and I haven't been this depressed about America since
the Civil War.

FRANKLIN:
ONCE I WAS A MAN
WITH DREAMS AND IDEALS …
NOW LOOK AT ME: I'M MONEY.
DIRTY, FILTHY MONEY …

(She uses his nose to sniff cocaine)

FRANKLIN: Whoa! *(He floats on the feeling for a
moment)* Everything in moderation.

(Waiter. Man#2, enters with champagne)

WAITER: Champagne?

FRANKLIN: Including moderation.

(He grabs a glass and drinks)

WOMAN:
IT TAKES MONEY!
MAN:
IT TAKES MONEY!
WAITER:
IT TAKES MONEY!
ALL 4:
IT TAKES MONEY!

(Blackout.)

(If you wish to break this into two acts, Act I would end here)

SCENE 10: A Hair Salon

(Scene begins in darkness)

FRANKLIN: Oh, my poor head. Where am I? The last thing I remember was being stuffed into a pocket. Now I seem to be in a purse. Hey, let me out. Don't you know who I am?

I'M MONEY.
THE ALMIGHTY DOLLAR.
PEOPLE ROUND THE WORLD ADORE ME …

Ohh, singing makes my head feel worse. It's awfully dark in here. What's this? *(Rattling sound)* Advil. Thank God! Now if only I had some water. Hey, let me out of here. *(Lights come on suddenly from above)* Thank you. That's much better.

(Lights reveal scene at hairdresser's. Congressman Cheezly's wife (played by Man #1 has just opened her purse to take out compact and lipstick. Man #2 is Francois)

WIFE: Francois, thank you for seeing me on such short notice.

FRANCOIS: For you, my darling, I move heaven and earth. What is your wish today?

WIFE: Congressman Cheezly and I are giving a big party this evening. For the governor of New York.

FRANKLIN: New York? Am I in New York now?

WIFE: It's a fundraiser for his re-election. And I'm chairing the committee.

FRANKLIN: Democracy is two wolves and a lamb voting on what to have for lunch. Do you mind if I help myself to some water?

WIFE: I got this money from my husband's pocket. He had to work late last night, and he was still sleeping when I left. He seems to be working late a lot these days.

FRANKLIN: Oh yes, Congressman Cheezly. It's all coming back to me. *(Pours a glass of water)*

WIFE: So I thought I'd create a new look to well ... rekindle his interest.

FRANKLIN: Life's tragedy is that we get old too soon and wise too late. *(Takes Advil)*

FRANCOIS: I understand completely, my darling. C'est bone!

FRANKLIN: C'est bone? C'est bone? *(To woman)*
I spent ten years in France as America's Ambassador. I speak French almost as well I speak English, and I must tell you, this man is about as French as a French fry.

WIFE: C'est bon, Francois. I put myself in your hands.

FRANKLIN: Beauty and folly are old companions.

(He sits in a chair and puts a wet towel over his head)

FRANCOIS: So ... I begin.

(Francois starts to cut woman's hair)

FRANCOIS:
IF I CALLED MYSELF A BARBER
I COULD CHARGE TWELVE BUCKS A HEAD.
BUT CALL ME A HAIRSTYLIST
I GET A HUNDRED BUCKS INSTEAD.

AND IF I GIVE THE STRONG IMPRESSION
THAT I MIGHT BE FRENCH AND GAY.
Oh! Quelle cheveux!
IT'S AMAZING WHAT SOME PEOPLE WILL PAY.

IF I "TAWKED" LIKE A NEW YAWKER,
THEY WOULD LET ME SWEEP THE FLOORS.
BUT A PRECIOUS FOREIGN ACCENT.
Café?
HAS THEM BANGING DOWN MY DOORS.

NOW COMBINE THAT WITH A MANNER
THAT'S BOTH FABULOUS AND FEY.
(Brandishing scissors) En garde!
AND IT'S AMAZING WHAT SOME PEOPLE
WILL PAY.

THEY'RE NOT PAYING FOR THEIR HAIR REMOVAL
THEY'RE PAYING FOR MY DEBONAIR APPROVAL.

You look like Bridget Bardot! … Or Catherine Deneuve, I
cannot decide.

FRANKLIN: If you ask me, she looks like Charles de Gaulle.

FRANCOIS:
THEY'RE NOT PAYING FOR MY SKILL
AT COLOR RINSING.
THEY'RE PAYING CAUSE MY MINCING
IS CONVINCING.

I WAS REALLY BORN IN FLUSHING
AND MY GIVEN NAME WAS FRANK.
THEN I MARRIED, HAD TWO CHILDREN
NEEDED MONEY IN THE BANK.

SO NOW I AM FRANCOIS,
THE TWIT THEY TREAT WITH AWE.
AND NOW THAT I SWISH
I CAN CHARGE WHAT I WISH.

IF I ACT LIKE I'M PORTRAYING THE MC IN CABARET,
OR AN OVERZEALOUS DANCER
IN A MATTHEW BOURNE BALLET,
IT'S AMAZING AND CONFOUNDING
AND FINANCIALLY ASTOUNDING
WHAT SOME WEALTHY, WORLDLY WOMEN …
(AND IT ISN'T JUST THE WOMEN) … WILL PAY.

FRANCOIS: Voila! *(Holds up large hand mirror to wife)*

WIFE: Oh, Francois. It's perfect. How do you say perfect in French?

FRANCOIS: Ah… what does it matter? You are a work of art in any language.

WIFE: *(Simpering)* You think so?

FRANKLIN: He who falls in love with himself will have no rivals.

WIFE: You're such a darling. Here. *(She gives him Franklin)*

FRANCOIS: I almost feel guilty taking your money.
(Grabs Franklin) Au revoir, ma cherie.

WIFE: Au revoir, Francois.

FRANCOIS: A bientot. *(She exits. Smartphone goes off. Looks at message. Suddenly talks with a Brooklyn accent)* Holy crap! *(Calls offstage)* Gloria, I have to go see a lawyer. It's an emergency. *(Grabs Franklin)*

FRANKLIN: I don't suppose you could leave me here? *(Gets pulled offstage)* No, I thought not.

(Vamp of It Takes Money into next scene)

SCENE 11: Law Office

(We see Francois with a female lawyer looking at a computer screen)

LAWYER: Let me get this straight. You want to sue another hairstylist for slander and defamation of character?

FRANCOIS: Exactly.

FRANKLIN: A female lawyer. How refreshing.

LAWYER: And what did he write that was defaming?

FRANCOIS: It's right there on his Facebook page. He "inned" me!

LAWYER: You mean outed?

FRANCOIS: No "inned." He says that I'm happily married and that I love my wife.

LAWYER: And that's bad?

FRANCOIS: No one will pay me $100 for a haircut again. Will you help me?

LAWYER: Everyone is entitled to legal representation. Even a man portraying a stereotype that manages to offend both the Gays and the French at the same time. However, I'm not sure you can sue anyone for telling the truth.

FRANKLIN: Have you seen the headlines recently?

FRANCOIS: But it's so unfair! We have to stop him somehow.

FRANKLIN: My advice: do good to your friends to keep them, to your enemies to win them. And believe me, if can you do good to John Adams, you can do good to anyone.

LAWYER: I believe my colleague gets his hair cut with this man. Let me have Jeff talk to him.

FRANCOIS: Great. I know this must sound silly.

LAWYER: That's all right. I know all about stereotypes. People assume that as a woman I'll be too emotional to represent them.

FRANKLIN: I don't believe in stereotypes. I prefer to hate people on a more personal basis.

FRANCOIS: Are you … too emotional?

LAWYER: *(Lashing out angrily)* God, no! Why would you say that?

FRANCOIS: What?

LAWYER: I was being sarcastic.

FRANCOIS: Ah.

FRANKLIN: Sarcasm is the lowest form of humor but the highest form of flattery. When I told Adams he should run for president, I was being sarcastic. You know how that turned out.

FRANCOIS: So how much will this cost me?

LAWYER: It shouldn't take long. A hundred dollar retainer should be fine.

FRANCOIS: Worth every penny. *(Gives her Franklin)* Thank you. So much. *(He exits)*

FRANKLIN: God works wonders now and then. Behold a lawyer and an honest man … I mean, person.

LAWYER: *(Calling offstage)* Jeff!

FRANKLIN: When I was a printer, I had a female business partner. Much better at the job than her husband. Looking back now, I can see we should have written "all men and women are created equal" to avoid any confusion. But we didn't. And for one very good reason: we were stupid.

(Jeff, played by Man #2, enters)

JEFF: Yes?

LAWYER: Jeff. *(Jeff enters)* I need you to take care of something for me. First thing tomorrow.

(Lawyer hands Franklin and papers to Jeff)

JEFF: Can it wait 'til the afternoon? Evan and I have a meeting with…

LAWYER: Oh, right. Afternoon will be fine. And Jeff … good luck.

(Vamp of It Takes Money a step higher)

SCENE 12: Adoption Agency

(Jeff and his partner, Evan, played by Man #1, are meeting with a woman at an adoption agency)

ARIETTA: Mr. and Mr. Priss.

JEFF: That's Price.

ARIETTA: Of course it is. And you wish to adopt a baby girl?

EVAN: That's right.

ARIETTA: *(Puts on glasses to look at application)* Hmm. Hmmm.

FRANKLIN: Bifocals! I invented those, you know. As well as the lightning rod, the Franklin stove, swim fins and the flexible urinary catheter. Most of the things I invented were to answer my own needs, including, unfortunately, the catheter.

(She puts down glasses)

ARIETTA: Dear, dear, dear.

FRANKLIN: *(Picking up glasses)* May I? *(Examines them)* I never patented my inventions. Could have made a fortune, but, to quote my autobiography, "… As we enjoy great advantages from the inventions of others, we should be glad of an opportunity to serve others by any invention of ours; and this we should do freely and generously."

EVAN: Is there a problem, Miss Hardcheck?

ARIETTA: Well, we have a limited number of babies. And we do want to make sure they go to the best homes.

JEFF: We both make an excellent living.

ARIETTA: I'm sure you do.

FRANKLIN: I can vouch for their character. I spent a lovely evening with them.

ARIETTA: And who would take care of the baby?

EVAN: I'm prepared to take time off, till she's ready for school.

ARIETTA: Are you? How nice.

FRANKLIN: They're going to turn one of the bedrooms into a nursery.

ARIETTA: Of course, we have to take your lifestyle into consideration.

JEFF: What does that mean?

ARIETTA: It means we give preference to married couples, naturally.

JEFF: We are married.

ARIETTA: Oh, please. *(Laughs)*

JEFF: According to the state of New York and our church.

ARIETTA: Your church? You mean Interfaith?

JEFF: That's right.

ARIETTA: Correct me if I'm wrong: that's one of those new-age churches that sees all faiths as equal. Brothers under the skin, so to speak.

JEFF: Yes, that's exactly what it is.

ARIETTA: If you don't mind my saying, I don't approve.

FRANKLIN: Any fool can criticize, condemn and complain. And most fools do.

EVAN: I do mind your saying.

JEFF: Evan, please …

EVAN: We're entitled to our own beliefs. The constitution says so.

FRANKLIN: That it does. I can quote the line verbatim since I happened to write it. "Congress shall make no law respecting an establishment of religion or prohibiting the free exercise thereof."

ARIETTA: Yes, well, thank you for coming in.

JEFF: That's it?

ARIETTA: I have all the information I need. Course these things take time to process. Sometimes years.

EVAN: Look, if there's anything we can do to speed things up, we'd be happy to pay extra.

JEFF: Evan …

ARIETTA: Are you attempting to bribe me?

JEFF: No, no, he didn't mean that at all.

FRANKLIN: It did sound like a bribe to me.

ARIETTA: How much are we talking about … hypothetically?

JEFF: I don't know. A hundred dollars?

FRANKLIN: Oh, no, please.

BABY WOMAN: It would have to be in cash.

JEFF: No problem. Here you are.

FRANKLIN: I'm sure she'd prefer it in nice, crisp twenties. And Jackson is far less fussy about the crowd he hangs out with.

ARIETTA: Just leave it on the desk. *(Franklin sits on desk)*

JEFF: Well, thank you. Thank you for your time.

ARIETTA: You'll be hearing from us. *(They exit)* Application … *(Stamps paper)* denied. *(Looks at Franklin)* Now what do I do with this? The Devil's money. Only one thing to do. *(Takes out matches)* Burn it!

~ **Ben** started the first fire department ~

FRANKLIN: Burn it? No! A penny saved is a penny earned. And a hundred dollars is even better. *(She starts chasing him around)* Save me! People like her are why I started the first fire department. Help!

(She grabs him. Starts to light match)

ARIETTA: No, I've got a better idea. *(Looks at watch)* Come with me, Benji. I'll show you a real church!

FRANKLIN: God help me! *(They exit)*

SCENE 13: A Church

(Preacher, played by Man #2. and wife, played by Man #1, enter.)

PREACHER: Brothers and sisters, welcome to our Friday afternoon service. At the Church of Eternal Conditional Love, every day is another chance for saving and redemption.

(Adoption Lady enters with Franklin)

FRANKLIN: *(To Adoption Lady)* Normally, I don't attend church. I think the most acceptable Service we can render to God is doing Good to his other Children. Which is why taking that nice couple's money …

PREACHER: Arietta, there's a seat for you right here in the front next to my wife. I'm so glad you're all here. Because God has a special message for you today. And He's asked me to preach it.

FRANKLIN: No one preaches better than the ant, and it says nothing.

PREACHER:
THERE IS ONE THING I FIRMLY BELIEVE.
IT IS BETTER TO GIVE THAN RECEIVE.
GROUP:
AMEN!
PREACHER:
WHAT'S A LITTLE BIT OF MONEY
WHEN THE LAND OF MILK AND HONEY
WILL BE YOUR FINAL REWARD?
GROUP:
OUR REWARD.

PREACHER:
IF YOU DON'T WANT TO WRITHE
DOWN IN HELL, YOU MUST TITHE
AND GIVE, GIVE, GIVE TO THE LORD.
GROUP:
WE MUST GIVE, GIVE, GIVE TO THE LORD.

PREACHER:
GOD IS WATCHING YOU NOW FROM ABOVE.
HE WILL WITNESS THE PROOF OF YOUR LOVE
GROUP:
AMEN!
PREACHER:
IF YOU WANT HIS PROTECTION
THEN IN THE NEXT COLLECTION,
GIVE ALL THAT YOU CAN AFFORD.
GROUP:
CAN AFFORD.
PREACHER:
AND IF TIMES NOW ARE HARD,
WE CAN TAKE A CREDIT CARD.
SO GIVE, GIVE, GIVE TO THE LORD.

GROUP:
YES GIVE, GIVE, GIVE TO THE LORD.

PREACHER: My wife, Louella, will now pass around
the collection plate. Can I get a witness?

ARIETTA:
OH THE WORLD IS A WICKED PLACE TODAY.
FULL OF MUSLIMS AND JEWS AND THE GAY.
GROUP:
GAY MEN!

PR&WIFE:
IF YOU WANT GOD TO SMITE THEM
WE NEED CASH TO FIGHT THEM
SO DECENCY CAN BE RESTORED
GROUP:
BE RESTORED.
PREACHER:
YES, WE NEED YOUR SUPPORT
TO DRAG THEM INTO COURT.
PR& WIFE:
SO GIVE, GIVE, GIVE TO THE LORD.

(Adoption Lady in rapture dances around with Preacher's wife and gives her Franklin)

WIFE:
WE MUST GIVE, GIVE, GIVE,
PREACHER:
YOU MUST GIVE, GIVE, GIVE.
ALL:
YES, GIVE, GIVE, GIVE TO THE LORD.

PREACHER:
GIVE ALL YOU CAN.
NO HOLDING BACK.
YOU KNOW YOU CAN.
GOD'S KEEPIN' TRACK.
ALL:
YES, GIVE, GIVE, GIVE TO THE LORD.

PREACHER: Thank you, sister. Have a lovely rest of your day.

(Pushes her out the door)

LOUELLA: (*Counting collection plate*) Eight hundred and twelve dollars. Not bad for a Friday.

PREACHER: Another day doing the Lord's good work. Of course, we can't give all of this to the deserving poor. Some of it has to be deducted to support our ministry.

LOUELLA: Yes. There's the mortgage on the house. (*She takes out some money*) The new car payments. (*More money*) And then we have to maintain ourselves in a lifestyle befitting our position in the community. (*More money*)

PREACHER: Hmm. That only leaves twelve dollars.

LOUELLA: Never mind. We'll give the poor something more precious than money. Our prayers.

PREACHER: Well said, darling. We'll pray for them tonight after dinner ... at Le Bernardin?

FRANKLIN: If men are so wicked with religion, what would they be without it.

PREACHER: As the Good Book says, "God helps those who help themselves."

FRANKLIN: Wait a minute. The Good Book didn't say that. I did.

PREACHER: The Book of Isaiah, I believe.

FRANKLIN: Poor Richard's Almanac.

PREACHER: The Bible has so many lessons for us.

FRANKLIN: A learned blockhead is a greater blockhead than an ignorant one.

PREACHER: Oh. look at the time. I better get to the bank.

(He starts out with Franklin as lights fade)

SCENE 14: A Bank

(Teller, played by Man #1, is standing at counter. Preacher enters with Franklin)

TELLER: Next.

PREACHER: Hello, Gene.

TELLER: Reverend, how's it goin'?

PREACHER: Rather well, in fact. I wanted to get this into my account before you close for the weekend.

TELLER: Eight hundred dollars?

PREACHER: People can be generous when you appeal to their better nature.

TELLER: *(Looks at Franklin)* Oh, this is one of those old hundreds. Don't see these much anymore.

PREACHER: Why not?

TELLER: Too easy to counterfeit. See this new hundred has a blue 3-D ribbon. And an inkwell that changes color from copper to green. Makes it harder to duplicate.

FRANKLIN: … And easier to ridicule.

(Franklin, as portrayed by woman, pops up)

NEW $100:
I'M MONEY
I'M THE NEWEST VERSION
FOCUS GROUPS THINK I'M A WINNER.
I'M DIFFICULT TO COUNTERFEIT.
PLUS SEXIER AND THINNER.

I'M ON THE MONEY, I'M ON THE MONEY … *(She exits)*

PREACHER: My God. You don't think this one is counterfeit, do you?

TELLER: No, no, looks okay. It's in pretty bad shape though.

FRANKLIN: I beg your pardon.

TELLER: A lot of wrinkles, frayed at the edges. And look at this. Someone wrote Jenny in the corner.

PREACHER: Does that mean you won't take it?

TELLER: No, we'll take it. Money's money.

FRANKLIN: There, you see. Nothing to worry about.

TELLER: We'll probably destroy it though.

FRANKLIN: What?

TELLER: We put all the worn-out banknotes in a special safe. Once a month the Central Bank collects them and give us new banknotes in their stead. So no one loses out.

FRANKLIN: Except the worn-out banknotes. I've heard enough. Shall we take our business elsewhere?

TELLER: Ah, I'll put this in petty cash for now. We're about to close.

FRANKLIN: Never leave till tomorrow what you can do today. Though in this case, I'm willing to make an exception.

TELLER: Here's your new balance.

PREACHER: Well! The Good Lord provides, doesn't he? *(He exits)*

TELLER: Easy for you to say, reverend. You don't work 8 hours a day 5 days a week just to keep your head above water.

FRANKLIN: Early to bed and early to rise … *(Teller slams drawer shut catching Franklin's hand)* Ahh! I can't believe you did that. I was only trying to help. I think it's broken. Or badly creased. Hard to say. *(Teller starts locking up and turning off lights. Franklin appeals to him)* I believe most of the miseries of mankind are caused by the false estimates they have of the value of things. I am all for doing good to the poor, but I think the best way to help is not making them easy in poverty but leading them out of it. *(Teller turns on iphone, puts buds in his ears)* Money has never made man happy, nor will it. The more of it one has, the more one wants. (*Teller laughs at something on screen, Ben looks*) Oh, for God's sake. I'm being ignored for a cat video. (*Teller presses app, heads out door singing "How did I fall" along with song on iphone, leaving Franklin alone.*) Might as well destroy me for all the good I'm doing.

BEN:
DOES ANYONE HEAR ME NOW?
I'M TALKING AS LOUD AS I CAN.
DOES ANYONE HEAR ME AVOW
THE THINGS I BELIEVED AS A MAN?

DOES ANYONE HEAR ME STRIVE
TO SAY WHAT NEEDS TO BE SAID?
IT'S HARD WHEN YOU'RE ALIVE.
IT'S HARDER WHEN YOU'RE DEAD.

PEOPLE HEARD ME WHEN I WROTE
POOR RICHARD'S ALMANAC,
WHEN I GAVE ADVICE AND TRIED
TO GAUGE THE WEATHER.

PEOPLE HEARD ME IN THE
CONTINENTAL CONGRESS
WHEN I TOLD THEM ALL THAT
WE MUST STAND TOGETHER.

PEOPLE HEARD ME WHEN I CALLED
FOR PUBLIC LIBRARIES
SO THE POOR WOULD HAVE
AN EQUAL CHANCE FOR LEARNING.

THEY HEARD ME WHEN I OFFERED THEM
THE LIGHTNING ROD,
WHOSE BENEFIT SAVED COUNTLESS
HOMES FROM BURNING.

~ Ben created the first public library ~

PEOPLE HEARD ME WHEN I FOUNDED
THE FIRST HOSPITAL,
TO TAKE CARE OF THE SICK AND THE INSANE.
AND WHEN I FOUNDED PENNSYLVANIA UNIVERSITY.
AH, BUT THAT WAS A TIME MORE CIVIL AND HUMANE.

(Montage of quotes are heard as if voices in Franklin's head. We hear the actual recorded quotes. Franklin tries to shut his ears and escape them: "People have got to know whether or not their president's a crook. Well, I am not a crook." "I'm gonna say this again. I did not have sexual relations with that

woman." "The concept of global warming was created by and for the Chinese." "Are you now or have you ever been a member of the Communist party?" "We have to pass the bill to find out what's in it. Away from the fog of controversy." "Rarely is the question asked: Is our children learning?" "Gay marriage should be between a man and a woman." "When you're a star, they let you do it." "When a President does it, it is not illegal." "I could stand in the middle of Fifth Avenue and shoot somebody and I wouldn't lose any voters.")

DOES ANYONE ELSE FEEL SHOCK
AT THE LEADERS WE NOW PICK?
DO THEY HEAR THE TICKING CLOCK
NOW THAT CLOCKS NO LONGER TICK?

DOES ANYONE HEAR ME NOW
OR KNOW WHAT I WAS FOR?
AND EVEN IF THEY DO SOMEHOW
DOES ANYONE CARE ANYMORE?
IN THIS WORLD OF I WANT MORE
AND MORE AND MORE …
DOES ANYONE HEAR ME NOW?

(Blackout)

<u>SCENE 15: Office of Bank CEO</u>

(CEO, played by Man #2, is practicing his putting. Speaks into intercom)

CEO: Miss Pennyworth, run downstairs and bring me $500 from petty cash, will you? Oh, and tell Granderson I need to see him. *(Back to putting)* If Mickelson sinks this putt on the 18th, he will win the Masters outright. A hush falls over the crowd. *(He misses the putt, then kicks it in with his foot)* It's good! He takes home the green jacket and one million dollars! *(He starts dancing around and imitating crowd noise)*

(Secretary enters with Franklin)

SECRETARY: Here you are, sir. $500 from petty cash.

FRANKLIN: Good lord! Just when you thought things couldn't get worse, I get him

CEO: What's this?

SEC: That's one of the old hundreds.

CEO: Well, it's in terrible shape.

FRANKLIN: *(Depressed)* You're telling me. Here. Here's a pair of scissors. Put me out of my misery.

SEC: That's the last hundred they had, sir.

FRANKLIN: I mean, what's the point anymore?

CEO: All right. Just leave it on the desk. There's a good girl. *(He pats her behind)*

SEC: You're not supposed to do that, Mr. Swagmore.

CEO: I know. I've had to take sensitivity training three times since joining this bank.   But since I won't be here much longer, I figured I'd go out with a bang. What about you, Miss Pennyworth? Do you think I should go out with a bang?

SEC: The worst wheel of the cart makes the most noise.

CEO: What was that?

FRANKLIN: What was that?

SEC: I said the worst wheel of the cart makes the most noise. It's a maxim by Ben Franklin.

FRANKLIN: She knows my sayings?

CEO: Oh, that blowhard.

FRANKLIN: Blowhard?

SEC: He also said, "He is ill-clothed, who is bare of virtue."

FRANKLIN: I did say that! My words exactly!

CEO: That's rather preachy, don't you think? From a man who was famous for his love affairs.

FRANKLIN: I was Ambassador to France for ten years. It was my duty to make friends there.

SEC: Will that be all, sir?

CEO: That will be all.

FRANKLIN: That will not be all. There's work to be done. I'll just put these scissors in a drawer.

(*Secretary exits*)

CEO: Now, where was I? Oh yes, doing nothing.

FRANKLIN: "The problem with doing nothing is you never know when you're finished." Nailed it!

(*Tom, the stockbroker from the first scene, played by Man #1, enters*)

TOM: You wished to see me, sir.

CEO: Yes, don't bother sitting down. This won't take long.

FRANKLIN: Haste makes ... Wait. Isn't that Mr. Hedge Fund from the strip club?

CEO: We have to let you go, Tom.

TOM: Let me go?

FRANKLIN: He seems nicer now that he's sober.

TOM: I made 20 million for this bank last year.

CEO: That was last year. Economy stinks right now.

TOM: We'll do better next year. I'll do better.

CEO: Won't be a next year. Corporate is closing down the whole division.

TOM: But you're in charge of the division.

CEO: Yes, so I'm in the same boat you are.

TOM: Is there … will there be some kind of compensation?

CEO: Well, of course. Oh, you mean for you. Two months' severance.

TOM: Two months?

CEO: And then there's unemployment insurance … I hear. And health insurance. For a while.

TOM: That's all I get? I gave nine years to this company. You've been here for two. What do you get?

CEO: Well, it's different for me, Tom. I'm important.

FRANKLIN: A man wrapped up in himself makes a very small bundle.

CEO:
I MADE A LOUSY CEO,
SO THEY'RE GONNA LET ME GO.
I MAY NEVER LAND ANOTHER JOB.
SO WHAT?

THE WAY THAT THIS WILL PLAY OUT.
I'LL GET A MASSIVE PAYOUT
SO I'LL NEVER HAVE TO BE A WORKING SLOB.
THAT'S WHAT.

I'M FALLIN' TO THE GROUND,
BUT I DON'T GIVE A HOOT.
I'LL LAND SAFE AND SOUND
WITH MY GOLDEN PARACHUTE.

I HAD A SHORT CAREER
BUT I'LL BE LONG ON LOOT.
CAUSE WHAT I'LL TAKE FROM HERE
IS MY GOLDEN PARACHUTE.

MY FRIENDS ON THE BOARD,
ALL WHOM I HELPED RECRUIT,
DECLARED THAT MY REWARD
IS A GOLDEN PARACHUTE.

YES, I'M OUT ON THE STREET,
BUT MY SEVERANCE IS A BEAUT.
I'M LANDING ON MY FEET
WITH MY GOLDEN PARACHUTE.

FOLKS MAY TALK BEHIND MY BACK,
BUT THEY'LL CUT A LOT OF SLACK
TO A MAN WHO CAN BUY AND SELL THEM.
I MAY BE FULL OF CRAP
BUT WHEN MY FINGERS SNAP,
YOU CAN BET THEY'LL DO WHAT I TELL THEM.

(Miss Pennywise enters with mail. CEO grabs her hand)

CEO: Miss Pennyworth, join me!

SEC: Mr. Swagmore!

FRANKLIN: Oh, please. Not the tango.

(They do a dance with CEO trying to hold her close, secretary trying to get away, and Franklin somehow in the middle. At one point, Franklin spins away along with CEO's wallet. Dance ends with secretary hitting CEO in the groin with his putter. He drops to his knees)

SEC: Your putter, sir.

CEO:
OOOH, PEOPLE FEEL SO BAD
WHEN THEY GET BOOT.
ME? I WON'T BE SAD
WITH MY GOLDEN PARACHUTE.

(He jumps to his feet)

YES, I'M OUT ON THE STREET,
BUT MY SEVERANCE IS A BEAUT.
I'M LANDING ON MY FEET
WITH MY GOLDEN PARACHUTE.
MY GOLDEN PARA …
HERE COMES THE LANDING.
MY GOLDEN PARASHHHHH-
Maybe I'll run for office
- SHOOT.

(He exits)

TOM: *(To Miss Pennyworth)* Look. He dropped his wallet. *(Opens it)* Six hundred, eight hundred … Bastard only has hundred dollar bills.

FRANKLIN: You have to give it back, Tom. Miss Pennyworth, tell him!

SEC: You have to give it back.

TOM: What? Why?

SEC: "There never was a truly great man that was not at the same time truly virtuous."

FRANKLIN: *(Finishing it with her)* …That was not at the same time truly virtuous." Oh my God! Don't you just love her!

TOM: Don't you get tired of quoting Ben Franklin?

SEC: Why would I get tired? The man was a genius.

FRANKLIN: Finally, someone who appreciates me. And not just because I'm made of money.

TOM I'm sorry. If Swagmore can be a bastard, so can I.

SEC: Oh, Tom.

FRANKLIN: Don't worry, Miss Pennyworth. Thanks to you, I'm back on the job and racking up overtime. *(They start to exit)* You know, Tom, I once said honesty is the best policy. Now what does that really mean … *(Lights fade)*

SCENE 16: Tom's Apartment

(Mover, played by Man #2, carries in ugly statue)

MOVER: Lady, where do you want this thing? …
Hey lady, it's heavy!

(Wife of stockbroker enters talking on cell phone)

WOMAN: Liz, I'll have to call back about that dress
order. I have to make an artistic decision. *(Hangs up)*
Put it over there, will you? Gently. It's worth a lot of
money. No, on second thought, try it over there.

(Tom enters with Franklin)

FRANKLIN: … So by policy, I didn't mean a document
or a contract, but a guide to living, so no matter what
happens …

TOM: Hello, Sterling.

STERLING: Tom, you're home early.

TOM: Yes. My boss called me into his office and …
what's that?

FRANKLIN: Never mind that. The important thing is …
Whoa! That's ugly.

STERLING: It's art, silly. I got it at Sotheby's.

TOM: How much?

STERLING: I got it for a steal. Three hundred
thousand dollars.

TOM: Three hundred thousand!!?

FRANKLIN: Beauty is in the eye of the beholder. I didn't actually say that one, but I should have.

TOM: You have to take it back.

STERLING: Don't be silly. It's worth twice that much.

TOM: Good, then sell it.

STERLING: You're a sweet man, Tom, but you know nothing about modern art. Whereas I've made it a lifetime study. I remember in college, my professors used to say … *(She continues to mime talking)*

FRANKLIN: In my day, modern art was a portrait by Gilbert Stuart. Of course, Stuart's most famous work is the portrait of Washington you see on the dollar bill. But I must tell you, it's not a good likeness. Because he'd lost all his teeth, Washington used to stuff his cheeks with cotton for pictures. Which made him look like a pompous chipmunk. My favorite painting is by Benjamin West. It's called Benjamin Franklin Drawing Electricity from the Sky, and depicts me flying a kite in a flowing red cape assisted by 5 naked cherubs. Now that's art!

MOVER: Lady?

STERLING: Oh. There will be fine. Tip the man, Tom, will you?

MOVER: Yes, Tom, tip the man.

TOM: How much?

STERLING: A hundred dollars should do it. *(Pushes Franklin toward the man, Tom grabs him back)*

TOM: I don't think so. Here's five.

MOVER: Gee, thanks. *(He exits)*

STERLING: When did you become so frugal?

TOM: Sterling, I lost my job today.

STERLING: You what?

TOM: They fired me.

STERLING: That's terrible.

TOM: Yes, it is. But if we could just …

STERLING: *(Same time)* How am I going to live?

TOM: Cut back on expenses for a … what did you say?

STERLING: Nothing. Just thinking out loud. We still have a lot in savings, don't we?

TOM: Well, not a lot. But enough to …

STERLING: And they're joint accounts?

TOM: Except for the IRA's. Look, I know this is hard for both of us. But maybe we could use this as a chance to spend more time together. Get to know each other again.

STERLING: Hmm. That's one idea. But I think it might help more if we took some time off.

TOM: From work?

STERLING: From each other. In fact, I think I'll start packing right away. (*She does so*)

TOM: What? Wait! You're leaving me now, when I need you the most?

STERLING: Let's be honest, Tom. There hasn't been any electricity between us for a long time.

FRANKLIN: That word again.

TOM: There hasn't?

STERLING: The only real attraction has been our mutual love of money, and now we don't even have that.

FRANKLIN: Of course, I didn't discover electricity. I merely proved that it was present in lightning. But I also coined many of the terms still used today. Words like "positive," "negative," "battery" and "charge."

TOM: You're leaving me because I don't have a job?

STERLING: Of course not. I'm leaving you because your lack of a job has caused me to see you in a different light.

FRANKLIN: Still it's ironic that "electricity" has become a metaphor for love, since electricity is predictable, easy to produce and highly safe if handled properly. Love is none of those things.

TOM: I never dreamed this could happen. Losing my job, my income, and now you. It's like my whole life has been an illusion.

FRANKLIN: There are three things extremely hard: steel, a diamond and to know one's self.

STERLING: Don't be so dramatic, Tom. These things happen.

STERLING:
NOT LONG AGO
OUR LIFE WAS BLISS.
AND RICH … IN EVERY WAY,
NOW SOMETHING'S MISSING …
WHEN WE KISS.
OUR LOVE IS SPENT … TODAY.

OVERNIGHT, OVERNIGHT,
WHAT WE HAD HAS TAKEN FLIGHT.
THE BONDS WE SHARED ARE GONE.
I'VE LOST ALL INTEREST OVERNIGHT,
AND YOU SEEM SO … WITHDRAWN.

OVERNIGHT, OVERNIGHT,
LOVE HAS TUMBLED FROM ITS HEIGHT,
AND WE MUST BOTH BE BRAVE.
I'D LIKE TO SAVE OUR MARRIAGE BUT …
THERE'S NOTHING THERE TO SAVE.

LOVE IS A STRANGE AND SURPRISING NOTION.
JUST WHEN NO ONE EXPECTS IT,
PEOPLE GO FROM THIS WEALTH … OF EMOTION
TO THE NEAREST EXIT.

OVERNIGHT, OVERNIGHT,
WHY PRETEND OR BE POLITE? *(Searches desk)*
I WEEP FOR WHAT WE LOST.
BUT I'M TAKING STOCK *(Puts papers into suitcase)*
AND OVERNIGHT
OUR LOVE MUST BEAR THE COST.

TOM: Wow. I just realized I've heard this song and dance before.

STERLING: What?

TOM: It was a faster tempo and it was sung by a stripper, but it's really the same song.

STERLING: Are you comparing me to a stripper?

TOM: Of course not. The stripper was kidding. (*He takes out Swagmore's wallet and looks at it*) And the worst part is, I'm as bad as you are.

STERLING: Goodbye, Tom! Have a nice life!

(She picks up statue in one hand, suitcase in another and starts out. Phone rings. She stops. Tom looks at caller ID)

TOM: (*Answering phone*) Mr Swagmore? I can guess why you're … What's that? The bank wants me to work in another division? Mergers and Acquisitions? Well, that's nice to hear.

(Sterling puts down her suitcase)

FRANKLIN: What you would seem to be, be really.

TOM: But … I've decided to take some time off.

(Sterling picks up suitcase and walks out, slamming the door)

TOM: Oh by the way. You dropped your wallet this afternoon and I found it. I'll bring it by tomorrow.

FRANKLIN: Now that's what I call a policy.

TOM:
I LOVED YOU ONCE
UPON A TIME.
I THOUGHT YOU LOVED ME TOO.
BUT WHEN LOVE CHANGES ON A DIME,
WAS IT EVER TRUE?

OVERNIGHT, OVERNIGHT,
WHITE IS BLACK AND BLACK IS WHITE.
THE DIE HAS BEEN RECAST.
AND NOW I SEE THE TRUTH AT LAST …

FRANKLIN: Wait a minute. Does this mean I'm going back to Swagmore?

(Music finishes last line of song)

SCENE 17: Shoeshine and Newspaper Stand

FLOYD: *(Played by Man #2)* Shoeshine! Magazines!
Newspapers! Read all about it. Congressman
Cheezly shot by wife.   *(Juanita enters)*

JUANITA: Rolling Stone, please.

FLOYD: Say, aren't you that singer?

JUANITA: What?

FLOYD: Wanda somethin'?

JUANITA: Juanita.

FLOYD: That's it. Knew it started with a "w." Saw
you last night on the late, late show.

JUANITA: Really?

FLOYD: Girl, you were good. You live in New York?

JUANITA: LA. I'm here to promote my new CD.

FLOYD: That right?   Look, if you need someone to show you
around … *(He moves closer to her)*

JUANITA: Thanks, I have a boyfriend. *(Moves away.
Presses buttons on iphone)* Jake, guess what?
Someone just recognized me on the street. Can you
believe it? … I miss you too, Jake. But it's only two
more days. And what's this I hear about you taking
my parents out to dinner? *(Floyd meanwhile exits
and come back on as CEO with Franklin. Juanita
bumps into him)* Oops, sorry.

CEO: Why can't you people watch where you're going?

FRANKLIN: Be not disturbed by trifles or by accidents, which … Juanita! Is that you? It's me, Ben. We jammed together at the studio.

JUANITA: Jake, you still there? *(She exits talking on phone)*

FRANKLIN: Are you still going out with Jake? *(To CEO)* She's still going out with Jake. Isn't that wonderful? She's going to be a big star.

CEO: Where's that shoe shine boy? Oh. *(Realizes he's the shoeshine boy too.)*

FLOYD: *(Changes back and forth, playing both parts)* Right here, sir. Name's Floyd.

FRANKLIN: Floyd? Oh dear.

CEO: Well, Floyd, let's give your shoeshine a try, shall we? And I'll take a copy of the Wall Street Journal. Can you change a hundred?

FLOYD: Yeah, no problem.

CEO: I lost this wallet a few days ago, and some idiot actually returned it to me. Had twelve hundred dollars in it.

FRANKLIN: There are so many maxims I could quote here, I don't even know where to start.

FLOYD: Oh my God. This bill!

CEO: What? Is it counterfeit?

FLOYD: No, it's … I know this bill. See the name in the corner? Jenny. I wrote that.

FRANKLIN: I remember.

CEO: Well, that's quite a coincidence.

FLOYD: Coincidence, hell. Comin' back to me like this. It's God tellin' me I should pay her back.

FRANKLIN: It's not God telling you. It's me: Never keep borrowed money an hour beyond the time you promised.

FLOYD: When I lost this hundred playin' poker, she threw me out for good. Learned my lesson though. No more gamblin'. 'Cept a course the lottery.

FRANKLIN: Actually, the lottery is …

FLOYD: *(Puts "Closed" sign up)* Gonna mail this back right now. Sooner I send it, the better I'll feel.

CEO: Wait a minute. What about my shoes?

FLOYD: Here. *(Hands him a few dollars)* Try the guy down the block.

FRANKLIN: *(As Floyd pulls him offstage)* A good conscience is a continual Christmas.

SCENE 18: A Bar

(Tom, the stockbroker, played by Man #1, is now a bartender. He's talking on his cell)

TOM: The apartment? She wants the apartment? I lived there before we ever met. Fine. *(Jenny enters with Franklin)* Tell her lawyer she can have the apartment.

FRANKLIN: A man between two lawyers is like a fish between two cats. Why it's Tom. Jenny, you remember Tom. He's the one who … Oh. Dear. Perhaps we should try the bar across the street.

TOM: I have to go. *(Turns off phone)* Sorry about that. What can I get you?

JENNY: A Sam Adams.

FRANKLIN: Sam Adams? Don't get me started.

JENNY: Woman trouble?

TOM: Now that I'm longer a stockbroker, my wife is divorcing me.

JENNY: A stockbroker? I thought you looked familiar.

TOM: We've met?

FRANKLIN: Here it comes.

JENNY: You probably don't recognize me with my clothes on. "WHO CARES IF YOU'RE FLUSH WITH MONEY, MY HEART IS PURE AND TRUE."

TOM: Oh ... oh! (*Raises his hand to his cheek*)

JENNY: You remembered. How sweet.

TOM: I'm sorry. I was drunk. You're not gonna slap me again, are you?

JENNY: Depends. What are you doing as a bartender?

TOM: I needed a change of scenery.

JENNY: So we have something in common. I left my job too.

TOM: Why?

JENNY: Too degrading.

TOM: Yeah, sorry about that.

JENNY: You were just one of the more blatant examples. I'm working at Macy's now. And taking dance class when I can.

TOM: You wanna be a dancer?

JENNY: I already am a dancer. Now I want to be a better dancer.

FRANKLIN: When you're finished changing, you're finished.

JENNY: No tips any more, but I like myself at the end of the day.

TOM: You know for some reason, as a bartender, I like myself better too. And I make enough to get by.

FRANKLIN: Who is rich? He that rejoices in his portion.

JENNY: Say, remember that hundred you gave me. I still have it. Or rather I lost it and got it back.

TOM: Really? How do you know it's the same bill?

JENNY: My ex-boyfriend wrote my name on it. *(Shows him)* Thought it would bring him luck.

TOM: Jenny. What do you know?

JENNY: What?

TOM: This is the third time I've seen this bill. Maybe it is lucky.

JENNY: Guess now's as good a time as ever to break it.

TOM: Save it. Drinks are on me.

JENNY: Thanks.

TOM: Name's Tom by the way. *(Shakes her hand)* Tom Granderson.

JENNY: Jenny. But I guess you know that.

TOM: You should invest that.

JENNY: A hundred dollars?

TOM: Gotta start somewhere.

JENNY: All right.   Invest it for me.

TOM: I didn't mean with me. I'm a bartender.

JENNY: So, you have experience. And working here, you probably get a lot of stock tips.

TOM: All right.   Let's see what I can do for you. Maybe I'll start my own financial consulting business. *(Writes on napkin)* Here.

JENNY: What's this?

TOM: Your receipt of deposit.

JENNY: On a cocktail napkin?

TOM: For now, that's my company stationery.

JENNY: Grey Goose. I like the name.

TOM: I might change it.   I should have your contact info too.

JENNY: Of course. *(Starts writing on cocktail napkin)*

TOM: I don't suppose you'd ever consider having dinner with your financial adviser, would you, Jenny?

JENNY: You're asking me out?

TOM: Yeah.

FRANKLIN: The Declaration doesn't guarantee happiness.
Only the right to pursue it. You have to catch it yourself.

JENNY: I should tell you, I have a child. I'm a single mom
with a child.

TOM: Ah ...

JENNY: Ah?

TOM: So what?   Life happens. We could eat in.
Order pizza. That's more my current budget anyway.

JENNY: I don't know, maybe. We'll see. *(Background
music changes to Juanita's song)* I love this song. Can
you turn it up?

TOM: Sure.   *(Music becomes louder)*

JUANITA:
I WASN'T THE BEST CHILD.
SOMETIMES I'D TELL A LIE.
I DROVE MY TEACHER'S WILD
I MADE MY MOTHER CRY.

JENNY: This singer is so good.

(She starts singing with the recording, then he joins in)

JENNY:
I NEVER GAVE MUCH HEED
WHEN FRIENDS WOULD GIVE ADVICE.
I NEVER SAW THEIR NEED,
I GUESS I PAID A PRICE.

TOM: You know you kinda sound like her.

JENNY: Really?

BOTH:
MY LIFE WAS TWISTING, STALLING.
I FELT LIKE I WAS FALLING
INTO AN ENDLESS SKY.
TELL ME, HOW WAS I TO KNOW
WHERE ALL OF THIS WOULD GO?
HOW DID I FALL SO HIGH?

(George Washington, played by Man #2, walks into the bar and sits down next to Franklin, who points to the couple)

FRANKLIN: If you would be loved, love others and be lovable.

GEORGE: Beware of foreign entanglements.

FRANKLIN: Do not fear mistakes. You will know failure. Continue to reach out.

GEORGE: Worry is the interest paid by those who borrow trouble.

FRANKLIN: Speak ill of no man, but speak all the good you know of everybody.

GEORGE: I cannot tell a lie.

FRANKLIN: Oh please, George. Not the cherry tree story again.

JEN&TOM:
HOW DID I FALL SO HIGH?

(Music changes to "Once I was a man")

FRANKLIN: Sometimes, George, I think we've grown too cynical. True, we've witnessed a lot of depressing things lately. Incredibly depressing. Monumentally depressing. But times like this … If these two can turn their lives around, anyone can. *(Picking out man in audience)* Well, maybe not him. But the rest of them. Look at them out there: a sea of honest faces; and here and there *(indicates someone)* the manifest potential for greatness. *(Lights fade on other three as Franklin sings to audience. Tom and Jenny exit)*

FRANKLIN:
LAST NIGHT I HAD THAT DREAM AGAIN.
THAT SAME OLD DREAM OF YOU.
I DREAMED ABOUT THAT MORNING, WHEN
THIS WORLD OF OURS WAS NEW.

WE CLIMBED AGAIN THAT SUNLIT HILL,
OUR HEARTS SO LIGHT AND FREE.
AND EVERYTHING WAS GREEN AND GOLD
AS FAR AS WE COULD SEE.

GEORGE:
THE RIVERS DANCED AND SPARKLED.
THE LIGHT SANG IN THE TREES.
AND FIELDS OF CORN AND COTTON
BECKONED IN THE BREEZE.

BOTH:
NO STORM CLOUDS THREATENED OVERHEAD.
WE SAW NO SPROUTS OF GREED.
FROM WHERE WE STOOD ABOVE THE FRAY,
IT SEEMED AS IF OUR DREAM THAT DAY,
MIGHT POSSIBLY SUCCEED.

(Tom and Jenny come back on as Lincoln and Hamilton)

ABE:
LIFE HASN'T ALWAYS GONE THE WAY
I WANTED IT TO GO.
ALEX:
BUT STILL THAT DREAM COMES BACK TO ME
WHENEVER I AM LOW.

BOTH:
WE CLIMB AGAIN THAT SUNLIT HILL,
OUR HEARTS SO LIGHT AND FREE.
ALL 4:
AND EVERYTHING IS GREEN AND GOLD
AS FAR AS WE CAN SEE.

THE MOUNTAINS SPEAK OF HEAVEN.
THE ROBINS SING OF SPRING.
AND WORDS OF HOPE AND PROMISE
ARE IN EVERY NOTE THEY SING.

THEN HAND IN HAND AND BOLD WITH YOUTH,
WE VENTURE DOWN THAT HILL.
LAST NIGHT I HAD THAT DREAM AGAIN.
I GUESS I ALWAYS WILL.

FRANKLIN:
THOUGH LIFE HAS NOT GONE
QUITE AS PLANNED.
WHEREVER I GO IN THIS LAND,
ALL 4:
THAT DREAM IS WITH ME STILL.

(Curtain. End of show)

BOW MUSIC

(After bows, they sing)

ALL 4:
I'M MONEY.
THE ALMIGHT DOLLAR.
PEOPLE ROUND THE WORLD ADORE ME.
BUT WHEN I SPEAK THE TRUTH TO POWER,
NO ONE SHOULD IGNORE ME.

GEORGE:
CAUSE I'M ON THE MONEY.
ABE:
I'M ON THE MONEY.
ALEX:
I'M ON THE MONEY.
BEN:
I'M ON THE MONEY.
ABE:
HEAR WHAT I SAID.
GEORGE:
SEE WHAT I DID.
ALEX:
LEARN WHAT I THOUGHT
BEN:
READ WHAT I WROTE
AND YOU WILL SURELY NOTE
ALL:
I'M ON THE MONEY.

ACKNOWLEDGEMENTS

The authors wish to thank the following people for their help and support launching our first Off-Broadway production:

Joan K. Soboslai, June September April, Michael Graff, Amy E. Gewirtz, Eri Nakano, Fred Rohan-Vargas, Jamie deRoy, Merrie L. Davis, 363 Grove Street LLC, Michael Kellogg, Michael Gosselin, Susan L. Cohen Visceral Entertainment LLC, Michael Chase Gosselin, Chinese Mother Jewish Daughter LLC, Michelle Poutre

Made in the USA
Middletown, DE
17 October 2020